SHINE/VARIANCE

For Dawnie,
still everything

'Think you're escaping and run into yourself. Longest way round is the shortest way home.'

James Joyce, *Ulysses*

'Please read this entire manual carefully before assembling this unit to avoid bodily injury and/or any property loss. If you do not understand these directions, or have any doubts about the safety of the installation, please call Tech Support.'

Metra Electronics Corporation,
Helios FML22 Manual

CONTENTS

DOLPHINS OF SEVILLE

FIONA WAS FINALLY ON HER first run of the holiday. She had the sea in her sights. It had not been straightforward to get to this point. To start with, she'd had to get her trainers past Ronan.

'*We recommend two twenty-kilo bags for families.* Oh sure. Family special. Click on that and there's another hundred euros for you,' he had said to the laptop when he was booking the flight. 'You *recommend*, yeah? I didn't come up the Liffey in a fucking wicker basket. One bag will do the two of us and the boys can carry theirs on.'

'That's not enough. And the boys won't manage,' Fiona said.

'Size of them, Fiona. Conor's fourteen, Liam's ten? Well able to carry their own weight in the world. Don't bring anything you can't carry on your back, as my Dad would say.'

'Like in the army?' she'd asked.

'Exactly! Now we're winning.'

This year, he was in charge of the holiday. He had chosen the one-bag option.

She pushed on, thinking of how Ronan pushed ahead of them all at check-in. He placed the bag on the scales. Twenty-two kilos.

'I'm sorry sir, but the maximum allowance is twenty kilos,' the agent said.

'That makes no sense. It weighed exactly twenty in the house. Your scales must be rigged.'

'You can pay for the extra weight,' the agent said.

'Oh I know I can, *Marta*,' he said, staring the agent down. 'You'd love that, wouldn't you? But that's not going to happen.'

He pulled the bag off the scales and opened it.

'Do you mind standing aside, while you ... do that,' Marta asked him.

As he dug through the layers, Fiona waited for Ronan to discover the contraband that had tipped the balance: her new trainers, bright blue, in the bottom of the bag. He held them up to her.

'Did these go in after I weighed and sealed? Who *does* that?'

'I only have my sandals,' said Conor.

'Me too. And only four pairs of jocks,' said Liam.

'Four is plenty. Be in your swimming gear most of the time anyway,' said Ronan.

He'd supervised their packing. Only essential items. But now there was a trainer crisis to contend with. And, it transpired, a further pair of unsanctioned sandals. He stared up at Fiona from the floor, inviting her to come up with a justification for this outrageous transgression.

'Give the trainers to me, I'll just wear them,' she said.

'Then we'd have to put those in,' he said, pointing at the shoes she was wearing. 'It just goes round and round.'

Ronan shoved a trainer into each of the boys' backpacks and approached Marta for a second weigh-in. Twenty-one kilos. Marta looked at him, then Fiona, and pushed the bag down the belt.

'We got away with it,' he said as they walked towards security. 'Free kilo. We're winning, lads.'

Fiona's trainers peered back at her from each of the dangerously overstuffed and open pockets of the boys' backpacks. They could easily fall out and separate. She pushed them back down as the boys stood in front of her in the boarding queue for Alicante.

'I bet you don't even get out for a run,' Ronan said.

She turned down onto the seafront, feeling light and untethered. She'd overcome the second obstacle: not loading up at breakfast. The strategy, Ronan had explained, was to go large at breakfast and last through to dinner. Unnecessary lunches and random drinks is how things rack up and get out of control, he'd explained. I like a lunch, Fiona had told him, when he presented his package choice. You don't know where you are after a big lunch, he said. He'd chosen half board in a complex that had been rated *good* on the review sites. Good is good, isn't it, he said. The sun shines just as bright on a two-star hotel. And the package was all inclusive. Except for lunch.

Ronan and the boys had stuck to the plan and gone large that morning. She'd watched blue syrup from pancakes ooze into neon scrambled eggs. Croissants were stacked on top of sausages. The plates supporting the weight could not be seen.

'This should keep us going for starters, lads,' Ronan said.

'Are you seriously going to eat all that?' she asked. 'It's a waste if you don't.'

'No it isn't, because it's free,' said Conor.

'Dad said take one of everything to see what we like, and then we can go back for the best things later. That's how you win,' said Liam.

'But you have three pancakes, Liam,' she said.

'Yeah, but I knew I'd like them.'

She took her turn at the trough, and came back with an apple and a yoghurt. And a bitter, tepid coffee.

'Sure that's ... why would you just get that?' Ronan asked as she sat back down. 'Jesus. Hotel one, Fiona zero.'

'I'm not hungry right now.'

'That going to do you to dinner, though?' he said.

'I don't feel well,' said Liam, not even close to completing his first round.

'Don't eat it if you don't want it,' Fiona said.

'He's grand. Pace yourself. Don't give up,' said Ronan.

Liam nodded and kept going.

'Thought I'd get out for a run, after this,' she said after a moment, waiting for this to land.

'In this heat?' asked Ronan.

'It's not that hot.'

'Do you even know where you're going?'

'I'll figure it out.'

'Well,' he said, dipping a sausage into his fried egg. 'Be careful.'

Ronan had been right about one thing: it was hot. She huffed along the promenade. Her muscles were roaring but she had to keep moving. Turning back now would be pointless, all she'd hear was that was short and was it worth the bother and I told you and bet you're hungry now, they stopped serving at eleven. But the crowd of tourists was getting too dense and she couldn't keep up a decent pace sidestepping buggies and shuffling old couples. She slowed to a half-jog and then a walk. Her mouth was dry and she felt the pressure of a headache forming on her temples. She'd forgotten to bring water, or money. Along the beachfront, she passed shops selling a menagerie of inflated beach toys. Grinning turtles and dolphins. Not the kind of places that would stand her credit. She kept moving until she couldn't take it anymore. She stopped in front of a café and pushed the door open. A small, less obvious place, she thought. Pale blue floorboards, white tables. No laminated *menu turistico* in the window. A young man came out from behind the counter.

'Good morning,' he said. 'For one?'

'Actually,' she said, 'I'm sorry, but all I want is a glass of water.'

'Just water?'

'Yes. I'm very sorry. See I was out running and I forgot ... If I could just get a glass of water?'

'Please, sit. It's no problem.'

She sat down and watched him walk towards the counter. When he returned, he was carrying a jug of water, and a coffee.

'Now, for you.'

'Oh I'm sorry, I didn't bring my wallet, so I couldn't ...' she said, though the coffee was something she very much could. Copper-coloured swirls around the circumference framed a delicate white leaf of foam. Even though she had not ordered it, it was exactly what she wanted.

'On the house. Give you a boost? For running?'

'You're very kind. Thank you.'

She poured a glass of water and drained it quickly, only touching the surface of her thirst. She refilled the glass and repeated the action. A third glass, and she felt herself returning to some equilibrium. And the coffee, well, it would be rude not to, if it was on the house. It delivered on the promise of its appearance. The hotel coffee was acrid and hateful. A considered, borderline *artful* flat white, a gift in a pleasant place: this was a world apart.

'This is really excellent coffee,' she said, as he passed her again. 'Thank you.'

'You are very welcome. You are from where?'

'Ireland. Dublin,' she replied.

'And this is your first time here?'

'Yes. Just got in last night.'

'You will like it. Lots of nice places.'

'Are you from here?'

'No. I'm from Seville. I come to here in the summer to work. My cousin is the owner.'

She studied his face. Copper-brown eyes, not unlike the colour of the coffee. If it was a Dulux paint card, they would be in the same row. Easy, open eyes. Some faces are closed tight with surveying eyes and unyielding mouths. But not this one.

'Seville. I've never been there,' she said.

'Oh, it's nice. Hot. Busy. But nice.'

He touched a picture on the wall. 'Main square there. Where all people meet and talk,' he said. His arm was extended as he made contact with the picture and she noticed the tattoo of a dolphin gliding up towards his shoulder, its head disappearing beneath the sleeve of his T-shirt.

'It looks beautiful. Look, I really should pay you for this,' she said, gesturing to her coffee.

'But you don't have any money, so that will be difficult? Unless you could work in the kitchen for some time?' She looked at him and he smiled. 'It is just a coffee. No worries.'

She glanced towards the blackboard on the wall. Specials written in chalk.

'You do food as well?'

'Oh, free coffee give you ideas?' he said, touching her shoulder.

'Ha, yes. No, I was just thinking, for another time.'

'We do very good food. But not until one. So you would have to run around for a long time while you are waiting.'

'Well maybe some other time while I'm here. I'll run past again and then I can pay you back.'

'Come in any time.'

'Bite me,' Ronan said, on the first night of Holiday Sex. It didn't happen on night one. He and the boys had watched an action movie on the dodgy stick he'd brought from home and inserted, with some fumbling, into the back of the hotel room TV. The movie was in Korean and the subtitles were half cut off. Doesn't matter, Ronan had said to the boys, it's mainly explosions. She fell asleep. There was no way it was going to be deferred to night three. So night two it was.

'I want you to bite me,' he said, when she didn't respond.

'No,' Fiona said.

'Why not? We're on holiday.'

'What's that got to do with biting you?'

'Something different.'

'I'll bite you and then what, you'll want to bite me?'

'If you want.'

'No thanks.'

There was no biting. Instead he positioned her in the three ways she accepted, arranging and rearranging her. One position, a few movements, then another position, and then the final third position and then it was time for him to go to sleep.

He lay there snoring. She read. A mosquito landed on his shoulder. She watched it advance down his arm, searching for a blood vessel. She watched it embed itself and gorge on him, filling and fattening itself.

'There you go now, Ronan,' she whispered.

Ronan was tall. He stood a good foot over her. That had counted for something when they met. He was a human shield, pushy and unafraid of the world. Whatever he wanted, he was going to get it. And in the early stages she could get him to want what she wanted. He pushed the world open for her. You want to go to Paris? Then we're going to Paris. You don't have a table, monsieur? We're not leaving until you do. Someone knocked into her when they were out, looked at her sideways, he was instant fists up and ready to take it outside.

That happened less now, because they went out less often, and people didn't look at her sideways or much of anyways. A shield can protect you, but also stop you seeing, or being seen. He shielded her from work. May as well quit your job. Stay at home and mind the boys. I make enough. If you get a job we're paying a child-minder and it's break-even then so what's the point. Simple maths, Fiona. The mornings could be very long, though, when the boys were in school. They grew out of things, ate into things, grew into him. He grew out, too. Once taut limbs had sagged. Everything was loosening, and tightening at the same time.

The boys had camps and clubs and subscriptions to many things. Outgoings increased, their income didn't. He had risen, reached his level, and was going no further. Need to take stock, Fiona, he'd explained. Can't keep living like rock stars can we? Let's switch to one of those

German discounters. We don't need all that deli mank. He'd never been into food anyway, he said. It's only fuel. He kept pushing with the same force, against smaller and smaller things. Waiters in Parisian restaurants went untroubled. Sea-view rooms went unoccupied. A garden room is grand, he said. We'll only be in the room at night. Who pays to look at the sea in the dark?

'Running woman, back again,' the waiter said as she arrived again the next day.

She smiled. 'Yes, back again. And this time I have money.'

'Money is good. And you would like?'

'A coffee again, please.'

'Like the one before, with milk?'

'Exactly like that one.'

She sat up at the counter to watch him make it. She watched him steam the milk and hold the pitcher over the cup, adjusting its height and angle. She looked at his face while he was doing it, those copper eyes locked in concentration. He set the coffee out in front of her. Another pattern. Today, the shape of a flower, petals folding into a white heart at its centre.

'Is that hard to do?' she asked, pointing at the flower.

'No, you can learn it from videos. On the internet.'

'Internet. Well, well.'

'I can show you how to do it,' he said. 'Come around and I will show you, if you like. A little latte art class, for you.'

'Why not. I'm on holiday.'

She stood up and went behind the counter. A picture of an attractive woman, younger than her, was taped to the coffee machine.

'Is that your girlfriend?' she found herself asking.

'No. It is my cousin's wife.'

She stood beside him, his hand guiding hers as they moved the milk pitcher together.

'You hold it like this, at an angle. Then you drop it down to get closer. Now you very gently, like this, you waggle it.'

She laughed. 'You wiggle it, you mean.'

'What is the difference?'

'I – I actually don't know.'

'So maybe it is waggle?'

'Maybe it is. Let's say it is.'

She looked at the cup. The pattern of a tree, dark branches cutting into a white circle. He'd made it, really, his hands guiding hers. But she was happy to be of assistance.

'You see?' he said.

A moment passed while they looked into the two cups. She picked up hers and he picked up the one they'd made together. They both drank, breaking the pattern. She waited for him to speak.

'You should really stay for lunch,' he said, tapping her hand with his index finger. 'You would like it.'

She looked at the specials board, not meeting his eyes. There were some very interesting-sounding dishes. Not included though. Not part of the all-inclusive deal she had been signed up for. She thought about Ronan's go-large-at-breakfast strategy. *You don't know where you are after a big lunch.* She was here. With this man. Maybe he lived upstairs, in a small room with other pictures of Seville, a guitar, a high window nobody could see into, books of Spanish poetry and a single bed. Her husband and boys were back at the hotel, maybe wondering where she was. Where had she got to.

'I would,' she said. 'I'd like to stay for a long, lovely lunch. But maybe another day.'

She kept a promise to Liam the following morning. Let's get up early, he had said to her, lying on her bed the night before. Let's get up early and go out, just you and me.

The light was still purple and turning as they walked. They listened to the birds.

'Do you think birds from Ireland and Spain would understand each other?' he asked her.

'I don't know. But that is a great question.'

'Do you like it here?' he asked.

'Yeah. Of course. Anywhere is nice on holiday, isn't it?'

'Do you like the food?'

'It's OK. I don't really like buffets.'

'I don't either,' he said. 'I'm too full all the time. I got sick yesterday when you were running.'

'Are you OK?'

'Yeah. Wasn't much. Don't tell Dad.'

'I won't.' She scooped his hair out of his brown eyes. You are not yet ruined, she thought. You're the last and the best of us. You're the one who should be shielded.

'What's your favourite food?' he asked her as they rounded and turned back to the hotel.

'I don't know. I like to try new things.'

'Are we going to do that here?'

'Hope so. Maybe you and me could go out some-where to eat? Something different. Not the hotel. Would you like that?' she asked.

Would you like to meet my son? Yeah, it's just the two of us. Yeah, we're thinking of moving somewhere else. Change things up a bit. What do you think, nice man? What is Seville like again?

'Yeah, maybe. See what Dad says,' said Liam.

'So how was it today?' Ronan asked her, when she returned from her fifth run of the holiday.

'Fine, yeah.'

'Are you going the same route, or mixing it up?'

'Same, pretty much.'

'Seems to take longer some days.'

'Well, I slow down sometimes. Just walk a bit along the beach.'

'Do you,' he said.

Could just say it, she thought. Here's my one-bag option. I'm not staying here anymore, Ronan. I'm going somewhere else. I'm going to stop running back and forth, and just go to where I want to be. And if people want to come and drag me out, let them try.

He picked up some brochures from beside his lilo and perused them.

'So there's the waterpark. Bus from the hotel.'

'Yeah, not for me,' she said.

'There's also a boat trip. They're included. Well, one or the other. Could go today?'

'I don't want to go on a boat.'

'Right. So what is it you do want, Fiona?'

'I don't want anything. Just, look if you want to do that stuff with the boys that's fine. I'm happy just to read my book.'

'Sure. Read your book. Go for runs. And focus on being miserable in your spare time.'

'Thanks a lot. Is that what you think?'

'Christ sake, it's obvious. We've come all this way. We've spent a lot of money. This is our main family holiday. And you're clearly hating it.'

'I'm not.'

'What is wrong with you?' he asked. 'When I want something, I just say it. When you want something, we all have to guess.'

She looked out at the boys in the water. Conor was holding Liam under. She shouted at him to stop.

'We're only messing, calm down woman,' Conor shouted back.

Ronan got up and pushed Conor under, with too much force. 'Don't call your mother woman,' Ronan shouted at him. Conor swam off to the other side of the pool, out of reach. His brother followed.

'He can be some prick when he wants,' Ronan said to Fiona.

The sun went behind a cloud. She let the heat go out of the moment with it. Let the air change and try something else, she thought.

'You know when you hear the name of a place, and you get a picture of what it's going to be like? Like someone says Provence, and you picture all purple light and sunflowers. Or Seville and you get a picture of a square in the evening, people gathered, yellow buildings,' she said.

'Never been to either,' he said.

'Me neither. But thinking about them gives you a picture. That's how you know what you want. Do you know what I mean?'

'So what was your picture for this place?' he asked.

'Tall buildings and kids screaming in a crowded pool.'

He looked at the tall buildings surrounding them and the crowded pool with kids, including theirs, screaming.

'I just thought, last few years, we've really gone over-board,' he said. 'And we should be, just a bit less – you know? Thinking long-term. We want a holiday home, some day, right? That's not going to drop out of the sky.'

'I know. We're being careful,' she said.

'A little restraint, you know? That's how we'll win.'

'In the long run. Right.'

He shook his head.

'Well, you'll be glad to hear it's nearly over. Just two full days left,' he said, looking over the brochures again.

'I tell you what I would really like to do,' she said. 'I would like to go out to lunch, on our last day.'

'Lunch? That's what you want?'

'Yes. That is what I want. I'm picturing a nice lunch, in a place on the seafront. A small non-touristy place. We can look out at the sea. We can order from a menu with specials written on a chalkboard.' Let's all go in together, she thought. Let something happen. Anything.

'It's just, it's not included,' Ronan said. 'It feels like a waste of—'

'And afterwards, we can come back here. And we can let the boys go off to the pool, for a while,' she said, and touched his arm.

'OK. If that's what it takes. Lunch on the last day.'

They shook on it. They looked out on the boys in the water. Conor was holding Liam down again. She decided to let it go. There wasn't going to be much more of this.

'If you got a tattoo, what would you get?' she asked him.

'I wouldn't,' he said.

'I'd get a dolphin,' she said.

★

On the last day they readied themselves for lunch, as agreed. She dressed in the good outfit she had packed. Her new yellow top. And her new sandals. Their first outing, on the last day.

'You're looking fancy,' he said.

They walked along the beachfront, her leading the way. 'This is the place,' she said.

She chose a table. The waiter came to them. He looked at her and at her husband and sons.

'I heard you do a great lunch here,' she said.

'Yes,' he replied. 'You heard correctly.'

They looked at the menus. Ronan read right to left, scanning the prices. 'This is, wow ... I mean, not exactly ...'

She looked at him.

'But this is what we're doing, so ...' he said.

The waiter came over to take their orders.

'If you were me, what would you go for?' she asked him.

Ronan looked at her, and then at the waiter. 'Fiona, I think we're well able to decide what we want,' he said.

'We have a lot of really great specials,' the waiter said, pointing to the chalkboard.

'Perfect,' she said. 'We'll get them. Just bring us all the specials.'

'We don't even know what they are,' said Ronan.

'That's why I want them,' she said.

Liam smiled at her. 'Mama is winning,' he said.

Plate after plate was presented. The kitchen had been generous. Chargrilled octopus with artichoke salad. Prawns with garlic and chorizo. Scallops in squid ink sauce. And a bottle of their most expensive white wine, straw yellow in the sunlight, the one he'd told her was from his grandfather's vineyard in Andalusia.

'Want to try the wine?' she asked Ronan, refilling her own glass.

'I don't drink white, you know that,' he said.

'Well, get something else then,' she said.

'I'll wait until we get back.' Drinks were included at the hotel.

Liam tried one of the prawns and liked it. Ronan toyed with an octopus tentacle and set it back down, focusing on the chorizo. Conor looked at his phone. Fiona showed no restraint. She devoured it all. They watched her work through every plate. They watched her drink the wine, all of it, not waiting for Ronan or the waiter to refill her glass.

'I want to go back to the hotel,' said Conor.

'You can do what you want,' she said. 'You go back to the buffet if you want. But I'm staying here. It's our last day, I'm having a nice lunch and I'm staying here.'

'We'll eat later,' Ronan said to the boys. 'Buffet opens at five.'

'I'm actually enjoying this,' said Liam.

Finally, she was finished. All of the specials, and all of the wine, of which she'd ordered another carafe (which was on the house, to Ronan's relief, and surprise).

The waiter came over. 'Some coffee?' he asked.

'I think we're good,' said Ronan.

'I would *love* a coffee, thank you, very much,' she said.

Ronan watched her as she stood up and went to the bathroom. She stopped at the counter on the way and watched him make the coffee, one more time.

'You make it so nicely,' she said. 'I will remember that. Will I come around and make one last one?'

'I think, perhaps not,' he said.

'Perhaps not ... because?'

'Well, your family is here, and ...'

She went around anyway. One last time. Who cares, she was on holiday. She was somewhere else. He let her take the milk, pour it as he had showed her. He looked at her, and at her husband, coming towards them. He came around the counter to join them.

The waiter moved off and lifted some cups onto a shelf. As he did so, Ronan saw the dolphin tattoo emerge from under his T-shirt sleeve. He looked at him, and his wife.

'Is this woman bothering you?' he asked the waiter, putting his arm around her.

'No, not at all,' he replied.

'I think she might be. What's your name?'

'Arno,' he said.

'Well, Arno,' said Ronan, putting his other arm around him, and applying equal pressure to Arno and Fiona. 'Meet Fiona. Though I suspect not for the first time.'

Fiona looked down at the coffee, her poor attempt at a leaf losing shape.

'There's nothing happening, it's not ...' she said.

'Ah, I know that,' said Ronan. 'Sure look at him, Fiona. You wouldn't be his type at all. That right, Arno?'

'I don't ...' Arno started.

'See, Arno. This happens sometimes, to my wife, on holidays. She runs too much, and then she throws some vino in on top of it, and in this heat – well she gets, a little – what would you say you get, Fiona?'

Fiona said nothing.

Ronan leaned in, lowering his voice and closing the space between the three of them. 'I'd say you get notions. You lose the run of yourself and you get notions. And you don't know where you are at all. Was she in to you every day, Arno? Stopping by for a coffee, telling you about her terrible life? Did she forget to mention she's married? With two boys?'

Ronan glanced towards his sons as he pulled Arno and Fiona's heads in closer to his.

'But as Fiona said. There's nothing happening here. Am I right?'

'You are right,' said Arno, looking down at the counter.

'Hear that Fiona? Nothing. And next year we'll go somewhere else on holiday. She'll probably throw googly eyes at some waiter or pool guy and embarrass herself again, Arno. Then we'll laugh again, and leave again, and on and on we go. That's the way, isn't it?'

Fiona put her head down. The pattern in the milk, the one she'd really remember, now had no discernible shape and was disintegrating on the surface.

'I wonder if we'll ever get a place in Spain,' she said into the space between them.

'Ah now. Cop on. We're more Wexford bound, I'd say,' said Ronan.

He loosened his grip on them.

'Now I think the best plan is for you to apologise to good old Arno here for making a bit of an eejit of yourself. And then we'll take the bill. I think you can leave the coffee off. And service. Seem fair enough?'

'Yes. That seems fair enough,' Arno said.

'Good man,' Ronan said, tapping Arno's arm.

'Dolphin tattoo. How very *continental*.' He laughed and turned to Fiona. 'For fuck's sake. Are you sixteen?'

There were a few hours left before the coach was due to pick them up. The boys had been sent ahead for a last go in the pool, Ronan answering their who-was-that questions with someone-Mama-used-to-know. He and Fiona walked along the promenade, his arm tight around her.

'So. You had your famous lunch. And you did your thing. But I know nothing happened. Again. So, that's that.'

'No, it isn't,' she said.

He corrected her in a low, weary voice. 'Yes, it is. Do you think I'm going back there to rip his stupid-looking dolphin arms off? Come on. I forgive you. It's nothing. See, I don't have to fight like that to—'

'Don't say it. Don't say *win*. I cannot fucking stand it anymore.'

'But we are winning. If you'd just stop this. We are winning.'

She stopped moving and leaned against the sea wall. 'We aren't, though.'

They looked at each other. She was done in by dolphins and wine. He was still reeling from what lunch had cost them.

'We aren't,' she said again.

He moved to hold her, tighter, but she pushed him away and walked on, back towards the hotel. She took off her sandals and started to run, bouncing off people on the promenade. She looked back to see if he was giving chase. But he was still leaning against the sea wall, holding his ground.

★

The Last Afternoon Holiday Sex did not materialise. She closed the door and lay on the bed, drifting in and out of sleep. She heard him return, maybe an hour later. She could hear him in the other room, shouting at the boys to pack their stuff and hurry up. She had already packed, that morning, ready to go, just one more run. He came into their bedroom. He was flinging his stuff into their bag. He was sweating and out of breath, as if he'd been running.

'Are you ready to go?' he said. 'We should go now.'

'Where did you go?' she asked.

'Doesn't matter. The coach is here. We have to go.'

They boarded the flight in darkness. She looked over at him, raising her eyebrows. He shrugged a cannot-confirm-or-deny. Is this what I have to do, she thought, to get you out of retirement and back in the ring? No problem, slugger. I can do this again and again. Until you're raging mad and back where I want you. Fight for me. Let's see what's left to win.

Her trainers remained on the balcony. Ronan had overlooked them on his final hurried sweep of the room. A maid put them with the rest of the lost property as their plane ascended.

WINGERS

IN MOST BORING ROOM EVER have Mam's phone but no signal she is in with Granda and not allowed in so nothing. TV on but it's horses and sound down and not allowed to change it so nothing. Go outside must be internet somewhere in this stupid place.

In the garden kicking ball against garage. Move around hold phone up no signal do they not have internet anywhere in this stupid country maybe just one computer in like the president's house and everyone gets five minutes a year. My Uncle sent to Mam: *You need to come back won't be long now.* I saw it first could have deleted and we wouldn't be here missing the final and I was in starting eleven for once but didn't delete and then on plane here and bus to nowhere place and now nothing but wait. Might be today might be tomorrow he's rallied he's failed he's taken a bite he's asking for you I hate this.

Now who are these two wearing Liverpool tops just wandering in. Sneak attack on me? Punch one of them I'm not going to come easily yeah smaller one in the neck then grab and do sleeper hold say back back or I will finish him. But big one bigger than me so don't.

'Are you Harry,' big one says.

No I'm your worst nightmare I'm unstoppable force watch this oh no he's got killer moves save us please we surrender no I will not save you not unless you tell me how to get internet.

'Yeah,' I say.

'I'm Daniel,' big one says. 'This is my stupid brother Rory.' They push each other.

Right cousins yeah. Not assassins. Didn't recognise. Just as well didn't unleash attack.

'You live in Manchester,' says Daniel looking at my top.

'Yeah.'

He makes a sucking-in noise.

'Can't believe we have a United fan in the family,' he says.

'Are you home because of Granda?' Rory says.

No dumbass here on holiday of a lifetime.

'Yeah, with my Mam,' I say.

We pass the ball around. I do three keepie-uppies and volley back to Rory.

'I did five once,' he says.

Five is nothing I can do twelve easy but better not show off.

'Do you want to go to the Astro,' says Daniel. 'Better than this stupid garden.'

They go over the fence and I follow. Are we allowed. Should we stay in the garden. Don't say this don't make them think you are a little baby. Should have told Mam promised don't wander off but we are there already now. Astro is full-size pitch ideal match conditions better than school.

'You go in goal,' Daniel says.

He tries to curl one past me but see it coming slo-mo dive oh wonderful stop how did he reach that he is keeping his team in this tournament no doubt.

'Skills, lads,' someone says.

Look over to sideline. A man and girl there.

'Will we get a match going?' the man says.

Don't know now don't know. Strangers might want to fight us and will cousins back me up can I count on them if we need to smash in some strange faces, will they have my back or double cross me don't know. Are they attackers or defenders.

'Yeah, sure,' Daniel says.

'Go on Michelle, get involved,' the man says to the girl.

Girl takes off her tracksuit top. She's wearing Man United away kit from last season. OK maybe one person on my side here.

'Not another one,' says Daniel.

'I'll ref,' says the man. 'Two on two. What are the teams?'

'Pretty obvious,' Rory says.

'Classic showdown so,' says the man.

The man takes off his jacket and also in United top. Three on two now. But he is not going to play. Wouldn't be fair teams. He shakes my hand like he's a match official.

'I'm Seamus,' he says. He puts his arms on the girl's shoulders. 'This is Michelle, and you are ...?'

'Harry.'

'I know these two bucks,' he says looking at cousins. 'But I don't think we've seen you on the Astro before, Harry?'

'No. I live in Manchester.'

He goes down on his knee looking right into my face.

'You're home for your Granda, aren't you? I'm sorry to hear now he's not well.'

You're sorry well try missing school final and playing with no skill cousins and no internet and now a girl.

'Where do you normally play?' he asks me.

'Left wing,' I say.

'I'd say you have the pace for it,' he says. 'Let's see what you've got.'

He throws the ball up. Michelle wins it and goes around Daniel easy he's chasing but he can't catch her. I make my run. She plays it long I run up the wing lands just in front of me perfectly weighted Daniel closing on me she's run into space I cross it over she slots it bottom left Liverpool caught badly at the back magnificent link-up one to savour.

Don't celebrate just nod at Michelle and she nods back like we are real pair of assassins even though she is in an away kit from last season and nobody from school saw it.

We do it again and again tearing through weak defence. Rory looks all red like he's going to cry.

'It's not fair,' he says.

What's not fair you're being outclassed she has a great touch want to say want maybe not to beat cousins by too much might get me later so glad when Seamus says that's full-time and brings us all into the middle.

'Good performance out there,' he says. 'All of you. Liverpool, solid stuff but you need to clear your lines. United, that was some great chemistry. Fantastic work rate, young man,' he says to me. Sounds like TV pundit and I like the way he is being serious it is serious. Cousins heads down saying nothing not gracious in defeat losing at home always hard on big clubs.

'The tradition at this pitch is the winning team does a lap of honour,' he says to me and Michelle.

Just me and her going around. She can run faster than me but for the lap of honour she is going slower because it's hard to run and talk and we just played a full match so we are not at peak fitness.

'You support United?' I say.

'Yeah.'

'Are they your Dad's team too?' I ask her.

'Yeah.'

'He's a good ref.'

'He did a course in it. He's a coach too.'

'Is he your coach?'

'Yeah, under elevens.'

Imagine having a Dad who is a coach all the extra skills practice you get no wonder such a good first touch.

'Did you ever go to Old Trafford?' she says.

'Just once.'

'Did your Dad bring you?'

'My Dad's not around.'

'Where is he?'

Not part of our lives not going to walk in the door no don't know where he is it's just us isn't that good enough for you more than a lot of people have please stop asking me please stop will you.

'Just not around,' I say.

'My Mam and Dad are separated,' she says. Don't know if saying it like you're not the only one stop moaning or you're not the only one it's OK. Could be either or both or just saying it.

'Who do you live with?'

'Mam in the week, Dad on weekends mainly.'

Don't know her Mam but Dad weekend seems like really good option for match day pre-training one-on-one time work on set pieces give her the edge.

When we get back around the pitch it is just her Dad.

'Where are Rory and Daniel?' I say.

'They went back to your Granda's house,' Seamus says. 'Do you know the way back yourself?'

Quitter loser Scousers just can't take the pressure at this level. Look over at the fences.

'It's that one there,' Seamus says, pointing.

'I know, yeah.'

He is doing keepie-uppies eighteen nineteen twenty now balancing on his back this is YouTube level.

'Do you want to practise some set pieces, Prince Harry, on loan to Ballyhaunis from Man United?'

Want a chance to work on skills but should go before someone comes looking for me.

'I better go back,' I say.

'Well, if you want a session sometime, we're out here most days.'

He puts one hand on my shoulder and the other on Michelle's.

'Quite the deadly duo,' he says.

Want to say to her she has really good pace and clinical finish and will definitely come back again but just say OK see you.

Daniel and Rory are in front room when I get back. Watching the horses still sound down what idiots why would you.

'Why didn't you wait for me?' I say.

'You were doing your show-off lap with your girlfriend,' Daniel says. 'We couldn't watch.'

'Shut up.'

'Oh, big man,' Rory says.

There is a plate of biscuits with two left and I eat them both and they can't stop me already in my mouth.

Mam comes to the door. I see her like five seconds a day here. She went into the room the day we got here and only comes out to tell me to go to bed or give her phone back or be quiet. Her hair is all tangled up on one side like someone was drawing her carefully and then got bored halfway through and just scribbled the rest.

'Come in and say goodnight to your Granda,' she says.

Go in. He looks like he has been in a World Wrestling smackdown with The Rock plus The Undertaker his hand is up in the air like he wants to say can I tap out of this ring can't take much more who will tap in for me.

'Hold his hand,' Mam says.

I do but it doesn't close around mine just stays in mid-air.

'Goodnight Granda,' I say but nothing.

'He's asleep now,' Mam says. 'So should you be. Go on in and get ready for bed.'

Sleeping in a room with tins of paint stacked up and ironing board and going to bed early while it's still bright this is just stupid. Want to stay awake until Mam comes in and can talk maybe tell her about the match at the Astro. But she is out in front room with Uncles. Think about my run and second goal when you hit it and you know this is going to fly in when you just make perfect connection and could I do it again tomorrow.

Still nothing no change bad night not long maybe today who knows. Cousins are at school so sitting on own watching now stupid golf sound down. Place just over fence much better idea.

Have the whole Astro to myself. Taking practice frees. Hear a voice from behind me.

'Very clean strike you have.'

I pass to Seamus and he volleys into top right like not even trying.

'Is your, is Michelle ...?'

'She might come over later,' he says. 'She's at school now.'

'Do you just come here on your own?'

'Sometimes, yeah. I have to practise too.'

'Michelle said you're a coach.'

'Yeah. Ballyhaunis under elevens. You'd be in my squad if you lived here, no question. On the wing. My old position.'

In his squad would be good place to be. Start on the wing Harry. Link up with Michelle great partnership all that extra training paid off. But I don't live here.

'Let's try some penalties?' he says. 'See if you can hold your nerve.' He goes in goal. 'Alright,' he says. 'Pick your spot and follow through.'

I try to curl top left but goes straight to him. Then try a little dink but sees it coming.

'You didn't really commit that time, Harry, did you?' he says.

'Not really.' Letting coach down start on the bench we'll get you on later sorry Harry next week try you in goal maybe. There's a lot of talent in this squad nobody's position is guaranteed thanks for coming out all the same.

'Do you know what might help,' he says. 'Watching some videos. Classic penalties. See how the pros do it.'

'I do that at home,' I say. 'But there's no internet here so I can't do it now.'

'You could come over and watch them at our house.'

'Do you have internet?'

'Course we do. Me and Michelle love watching videos of great goals. You could come over. If you want.'

First not totally terrible thing anyone has said since we got here.

'You can see our house from here,' he says pointing across to other side of Astro. 'Sure you can be back again in five minutes.'

Red door. United red. Classic.

'I'd say you're thirsty now,' he says. 'Go on in there and I'll get you something.'

TV is massive and Xbox and loads of games. We are back in modern era. He gives me a can of Coke and a Twix.

'Lunch of champions,' he says. 'Don't rat on me now to your mother. I'm sure she'll have a proper dinner for you later.'

Mainly takeaways since I got here fun first few days but sick of it now even chips are boring now. He sees me looking at the games.

'Are you more of a Call of Duty or Assassin's Creed man? I'm going to guess ...' He guesses right. I start playing. 'So you're a sniper and a winger. Great combination,' he says.

Keep shooting. This is the final stand and this one is for all of the people you bastards hurt and killed and I am going to take you down and show no mercy and you will be sorry for what you did.

'And how is your Mam?' he says.

'She's OK.'

'I knew her in school. We were in the same class.' I get killed and back to the start of the mission and have to kill all over again.

'Michelle said your, Dad wasn't ...'

'It's just me and Mam,' I say. Say quickly always and then something else. Say something else. So what lots of people don't have a Dad let's not have a cry about it man up if that's all it takes to make you cry you've more knocks coming in life than that I can tell you.

'When did you start supporting United?' I say.

'When I was about your age,' he says and goes over to the bookshelf. 'A devotee such as yourself will appreciate this,' he says. *Panini Soccer Annual 1982*. He hands it to me. 'I bet you collect these, what are they called now, Match Attax?'

Got 364 of them need twelve swaps for full set just twelve more.

'Yeah,' I say.

'Michelle has them too. I'm a bit more old-school. This is my collection,' he says. I turn the pages. Cards of legends all long hair and shrunken shorts. 'Man United first team back then, I'd rank them up there with the best.' He points to a sticker. 'Know this buck?'

Olden days player smiling posing one knee on ball.

'No,' I say. Don't recognise name on the sticker.

'He was a winger like yourself. Nippy and clever. Not a show-off. Connected things, created chances. Intelligent reader of the game. Shame how it ended.'

'How what ended?'

'Horrible tackle. Career ending. Done at twenty-one. He's a manager in the Scottish League now.' He is looking at the picture and shaking his head.

'That's terrible,' I say. Imagine ending up in Scottish League.

'He was a big lad, just came down on his own leg too hard. Wouldn't happen to you. Size of you, you'll stay upright in any challenge, I'd say. Use your size to your advantage.'

Saying I am small I know I am small for my age but he is saying it like it is good.

'Well. Listen. I have to pick Michelle up from her mother's. It's pizza night.'

'OK. Yeah.'

'Actually if you want to – just hang out with us, you're more than welcome,' he says.

I said I would go back and would not wander off. Though would like to be more than welcome. Could run home and say is it OK if I. But I can already hear the answer.

'I could phone your ... no. Look. Actually. Let's – another time, chief,' he says.

Please don't be like every grown-up say one thing then change and forget and never do it. Please don't be one of them you are better you seem like a good one.

'Maybe we'll see you on the Astro tomorrow,' he says. 'Then after you can come back here and you can play some more.'

'Yeah maybe.'

Definitely.

Back across Astro amazing run with zombie apocalypse chasing me how does he hold on to the ball under such pressure just over fence before flesh eaters grab my leg and in time to turn and score into garage wall.

Mam is standing at the back door smoking.

'Where were you?' she says.

Why smoking again? That was all supposed to be in the bin after him and him and odd one OK but can see like five or six butts on the ground. Don't say anything leave it not fight now.

'I was on the Astro with some boys,' I say.

'We are not here on our holidays,' Mam says.

No we are a thousand per cent not. Though today felt more like I was.

'Your Granda is very bad now,' she says.

'Will I go in to him?'

'No. He's sleeping.'

She lights another. Not hiding from me like usually out the back then brushing teeth and I call for her and smell it as if I don't know I'm not stupid.

'Do you know someone called Seamus, from your school?' I say.

She looks at me like I've said a bad word.

'Seamus Brophy?'

'I don't know his second name. He's like a coach.'

'Seamus Brophy. What about him?'

'I met him. On the Astro. He was playing football with his daughter and they let me play.'

'When.'

'Yesterday.'

'What was he saying.'

'Nothing. He just said he knew you in school.'

She blows out a blue cloud. 'Yeah. I knew him.' She says it like that was not a good thing.

'He's good at football,' I say.

'Oh, he was mister fantastic when he was sixteen. Or thought he was.' Still seems mister pretty great to me but don't say this. 'Suppose he was telling you about his trial.'

'What trial?' Trial like in trouble? What could he be in trouble for?

'Wolves. Some scout saw him and off he went. Didn't even do his leaving cert. His poor parents, God rest them, thought it was great news.'

'He played for Wolves?' Why would he not tell me this? Wolves very far from United but still.

'No. He *tried out* for Wolves. He never played for them.'

'But he's good at football.'

'Good for a forty-year-old in Ballyhaunis.'

What does she know about football never been to a match never taken me. That one man one time had tickets and was a bad match scoreless and then took me to the pub after and he was just getting drunk yeah thanks a lot got me home and heard them shouting when I was under the covers and that was that never saw him again we don't talk about him.

'He went into their academy and it was all going to be great things, then after a couple of months they dropped him and he skittered back here and went into his room in his mother's house. And I don't think he's ever really come out, only to bury his parents and marry Eileen Byrne and then he mucked that up too.'

This not a good time to mention house visit and Xbox and legends sticker album. If I had his room I would never come out either but don't say this.

'He was asking, just about Granda and stuff.'

'So you were chatting away to a complete stranger.'

'No. I wasn't really talking to him,' I say. Also not a stranger if she knows him. 'We were just, messing about. On the Astro.'

'Messing about. That's his specialty alright.'

I know she is tired and all Granda stuff but just being not nice and want her to say good things instead of being so angry all the time say something good.

'What's so bad about him,' I say.

'There's nothing bad about him. There's nothing anything about him.'

'He was at Wolves. That's not nothing.'

She leans in and has the hard quiet voice for when serious advice or trouble. 'Tell you what now. You think he's something, do you? Living in his parents' house, running his Dad's butchers. Does that sound like a great life to you?'

'I don't know since I don't have a Dad, yeah?'

'Don't get smart with me now.'

'He's a good coach. He was encouraging me. He said I was good.'

'He'll have you dreaming you're on your way to Wolves next.'

'Dreaming is bad, is it? Getting a trial is bad? What do you do that's any better?'

'I have a job, Harry. A real job. How do you think we pay for all this?' she says, pulling at my United top.

'You are always so gloomy when you come home from work. I'm not going to get a job like you.'

'Yeah, well, everyone has to work. You're not going to end up a Seamus. Stay away from him now.'

I know I won't end up like him no way I would get a chance at a major club I'm not that good. Small is not good I know he was just being nice to me. You can be not the biggest but you can't be the smallest.

'He said I can practise with him tomorrow. Him and Michelle. He said.'

'And I'm saying no. Cop on. What are we here for? Or have you forgotten?'

'You are so mean.'

'I am tired.'

'You always say that when you are being mean.'

'I am not going to answer that,' she says, and lights another.

I am in bed and making list of things not good one no Dad two angry Mam who doesn't let me do anything I want to do except what she wants to do and three not even allowed to train now does she think I am just going to go along with everything I can't wait to get older and move out and if I did get a trial I would not invite her to any matches.

I am pulled from bed it's time he's going I am in here looking at him room full bring Harry up one last look Mam says. I look in his eye open sharp looking into mine maybe when you go your eyes come bursting out of your head and fly out the window and then can go anywhere into clouds looking down haha see you later losers I'm off. He's gone someone says he's gone and then the crying and Mam holding on to him all Uncles crowding in and I am at the back now. I look at Mam and she looks at me angry like I did something. Harry you should go out now one of the Uncles says. You don't need to be in here. Means don't want me in here I'm too small to see this but I see it Mam has no Dad am thinking now we are same and you will see what it's like. Go into front room but don't want to sit quietly wait there's nothing to wait for now. Nobody will notice if I just go so go. Into garden through fence onto Astro keep going even though it's lashing rain running on over across why don't know why there but want to that's why.

You should not go to strangers' houses you should not wander off and it is very early in the morning might not even be up but do not care about any of this now.

'Harry. Are you OK?' Seamus says when he unlocks the door. He is in shorts and T-shirt.

'Were you asleep?'

'No no,' he says but grown-ups always lie when you ask them this and when you ask them most things don't be one of them please Seamus.

'You were.'

'I was, yeah. But don't worry about it, man.' He looks at me dripping on the doorstep. 'Jeez, you're soaked. Come in out of this.'

Standing in the hall and shaking a bit from the rain and the run. He's back with massive towel like we're going to the beach. He puts the towel over me and starts rubbing my head I am a wet dog covered warm safe.

'My Granda is dead,' I say.

'Ah Jesus. I'm so sorry Harry. Your poor Mam. When did he …?'

'Just now.' He puts his hands on my shoulders. He looks at me. Say something else. Something good now go somewhere else. 'Mam said you played for Wolves.'

'Oh. Yeah. God, she remembers that? That was a while ago.'

'But you didn't stay.'

'No.'

'Why not?'

'Ah.' He is folding up the towel and looking away like grown-ups do when they are about to lie. 'I didn't like the environment, to be honest. It's different, you know. At that level. I was a bit young, you know. I was only seventeen. I missed home, you know yourself.'

Football is more important than home why would he say this it is not true don't believe him don't be a liar and mean tell me.

'But why didn't you stay? Really.'

'Did my knee in, chief. Silly, in training. Fifty-fifty ball and I went for it, got caught badly. I was going to be out for months and – look at that level, if you're not a hundred per cent, well. There's plenty of others lining up. Wasn't their fault, it's a business and –' He puts his hands up in the air like that's that.

So not his fault was not dropped he was going for it.

'I'm sorry,' I say.

'Ah listen. That was years ago. Don't you be sorry. I'm not. It was a great opportunity.'

Created opportunities took chances tried Mam see actually tried.

'What else did your Mam say? About me.'

'Oh nothing. Just that you ... went there.' Am looking at ground and feeling hot and red.

'I bet she said more than that.'

'She's really mean to me.'

'Harry. Her father just died. Come on now. That's not fair.'

'Once she had a boyfriend and he hit me.'

'That's. That's shocking. Who would do that?'

He didn't hit me just shouted at me after the match because I wanted to go home would have hit me could see in his eyes. Lies are bad I know but want him to take care of me take me under his wing one-on-one. Mam says not true things all the time like your Dad wasn't a good man we are fine just two of us but two is not a team.

'Do you get any stick at school? About, your, you know ... Dad and not ...'

'Sometimes. People call me Halfway Harry. Because I'm small.' Small and halfway to nowhere run half the pitch if you'd let me if you'd pick me.

He is on his knees and face close into mine and arms on my shoulder.

'Harry. I'll tell you this now. People think they can have a go at you. Show them you're well able to fight back. Because you are. And if anyone ever says anything to you, or does a bad thing to you, you tell them that you know Seamus Brophy, ex-Wolves, you're in his gang, and they're on his list. Say you're on very good terms with the Butcher of Ballyhaunis. That'll shut them up.'

'OK,' I say. Want to say come to Manchester or I could stay here. Mam could like you and what is so wrong take chances. I want to get back under towel and stay. But can't. Shouldn't have come. Can't just run. Hold your position don't drift offside.

Michelle comes down the stairs. She looks at me and her Dad like she is trying to figure out a hard sum.

'What are you doing here,' she says.

'It's OK, Michelle. We were just having a chat,' her Dad says. 'He's just a bit upset. His Granda's after dying.'

'What are you doing here,' she says again.

Stay out of it stupid girl but she is right I should not be here find somewhere else to belong leave back over Astro. No ball no opportunity to strike just running back.

Cousins are in front room when I get back.

'Granda is dead. Where were you?' Daniel says.

'I know he's dead. I was there. Which you were not.'

I can be mean too. If you don't stand up then people stand on you push you down not taking this from you not from you dicks.

'Your Mam wants you,' Rory says.

No she doesn't. Maybe she is wondering where I am. Not same thing.

★

In the room with everyone coming in signing the book looking at Granda he looks very peaceful doesn't he no he looks like he's made of wax sorry now sorry for your troubles shaking my hand why are you saying sorry you didn't do anything I don't have troubles maybe you do but my only trouble is I want to take off this tight stupid jacket and shirt and go outside but I am not allowed. Everything is slow-motion now. There is just sitting and quiet talking and do you want a sandwich. After we go to the hotel. People are all loose and laughing like mass finally over and now they can just be normal. I am allowed to take off my jacket and I put it on the chair and am looking down at Mam's phone and someone taps me on the knee.

'There he is,' Seamus says to me. Michelle is with him.

He shakes my hand and it is solid firm good grip. He nods to Michelle and he makes her do it too but it's all loose and weird and neither of us want to. Mam comes over to us.

'Jeez, Sinead. I'm sorry now,' Seamus says, and hugs her.

'Thanks Seamus,' she says.

'I'm ... he was a great man. I'd call in to him. He'd tell me about you.'

'Not much to tell now,' Mam says doing the thing where she looks down and wants to say nothing and just go.

'You're looking well, anyway,' he says.

She says nothing in the place where you are supposed to say so are you or whatever.

He puts his hand on my shoulder. 'And this lad. Great little footballer. We had a few kickabouts, you know, Michelle and myself, and the cousins, hope that's OK ...'

Four of us standing there. If you walked in the door and saw us you'd think well obviously family. Obviously.

'Yeah, well. Thanks for keeping him ... occupied,' Mam says.

Come on look Mam here is a good opportunity come on will you and why not do you have any better ideas.

'Maybe we could have another kickabout before we go,' I say.

'I don't think there will be time, Harry,' Mam says.

'We're not going until tomorrow. Could do it tonight. Or, now.'

'No.'

'Next time, Harry,' Seamus says.

'Or you could visit us in Manchester,' I say.

'Harry, please. Will you stop. Sorry, Seamus. He doesn't know when to stop.'

'He's no bother at all.' He is taking money out of his pocket and putting his hand out to me.

'No need for that,' Mam says, pushing his hand back. Getting in the way and blocking things.

'It's nothing, just buy some Match Attax, or something,' he says, and puts it in my jacket pocket.

She has her I'm too tired to stop this face.

'Remember what I said now,' he says.

'Said about what,' Mam says.

'About committing when you strike,' I say and want to say I will remember but he's gone off talking to someone else and I am being dragged over to cousins.

It is the last morning she lied again there is time for one more go, we are not leaving for an hour. She is packing our stuff.

'Harry, will you come out of the way.' I am annoying her while she packs I'm doing it on purpose so she might tell me to go.

'Can I just go and play for a bit? On the Astro.'

'You have half an hour. Do not make me come looking.'

One more chance but he's not there. Michelle is taking shots not really person I want to see not the right set-up do not want to go up against her but no choice can't just run off.

'Want to take some shots on me?' I say to her.

'Yeah, OK.'

I go in goal for her. I've got a read on her now can tell which way she's going to go. Top left, saw it coming. Don't be too good in goals or will get stuck there.

'Where's your Dad?' I ask.

'At home.'

Could go over say bye and thanks and I'll remember what you said and maybe don't know keep in touch some way he could text Mam or connect on Xbox. But stupid idea why would he want that cop on.

'Why did you come to our house?' she says.

'What do you mean?'

'In the morning. After your Granda died.'

'Don't know. Was just ... I don't really know.'

'Do you wish he was your Dad? Because he's not.'

Does she think I'm dumb. I know that. Are you jealous? Is that your problem? Because I have a better touch than you and if I lived here I'd take your spot on the under elevens he basically told me that.

'I am better at football than you,' I say.

'You're not. My Dad says you lack pace.'

'He said that so you wouldn't feel bad. He said you were not good and you only get to play because he's the coach.'

'No, he didn't.'

'Face it. You are never going to make it,' I say.

'You think you have skills but you are too small to be a professional,' she says. 'That's what he said.'

I punch her arm. I know you are not supposed to punch a person or a girl but she is starting this and what am I supposed to do just take it just let her? Stand up for yourself. I push her over onto the ground. I want to push her eyeballs into her head and pull her tongue out and crush her skull.

'You are a liar,' I say to her. 'He didn't say that.'

'You are a nothing,' she says. 'I am telling my Dad you hit me.'

She's the nothing. Don't tell him. Don't rat on me. You drew the foul it is your fault. She is bigger than me though and gets up and punches me back. Ready for full out attack but 'Get in here now,' I hear from the fence. Mam is calling me. Michelle runs off before I can tell her what a fucking stupid idiot bitch she is. I want to shout but Mam is listening and Michelle is already across the pitch not fair someone so stupid has that pace and now going to tell her Dad see he's nothing he's useless you were right.

Mam is giving me water in the kitchen and dabbing my eye I'm fine leave me alone. Want to tell Michelle I'm sorry I know you are good and now your Dad probably hates me and I am the one going on his list of bad people and I'm not as fast as you and I don't care if I don't get a trial just don't tell him I hit you. But that's gone now no chance.

'Fighting with a girl. Is that how you show people what you're like? Is it?'

'She started it.'

'Why do you – why can you not just listen? I told you. Stop. Wandering. Off.' She slaps me on the arm on the Off. 'This is all fucking Seamus. I should have known better than to let you near him.'

'He is way better than you. I wish I could live with him.'

She slaps me in the face and it is still stinging in the taxi.

We are on the way to the airport. Mam is not talking. I am wearing the jacket from the funeral because Mam packed my United top. I take out the money he put in the pocket and look again at what he gave me wrapped inside it. I look over at Mam but she is looking out the window.

Open my Match Attax album and put my new player in with the rest of the United squad. He cut it out of his album and it's not a Match Attax and not current squad but I don't care it's a legend it's a classic and deserves to be in there on the wing where he belongs. Connected things made opportunities. One of the good ones. See Mam? See Michelle? Would you give this to someone if you didn't think they were good? Would you cut out your best one and write *keep up the pace Harry, all the best Seamus*, would you?

'When we get back, we're going to cut down on your football time,' Mam says in the car. 'It's making you aggressive. You need to do something else. You're obsessed. It's wrong.'

It's not wrong. Seamus is not wrong. She's wrong. She doesn't know that when you have an opportunity you have to take it create chances. That's what wingers do. Team before family. United.

RIPTIDE

THEY'RE COMING INTO THE CAFÉ, these three, in a row. A tiny private procession. I don't like how the man is handling the woman – his wife, I assume, from the way he is pulling her along. He's leading her to the counter by the hand like a child. The girl – their daughter, I assume, from the way she is not looking at either of them – follows head down. Soaked, the three of them. Brought the outside in. They are none of my business but I am close enough to hear them. That's not my fault. It's a small place. If you want privacy, stay in bed.

'What do you want,' the man says to his wife at the counter, staring into the display, wiping rain from his eyes.

'I don't know,' she says.

'You want a sandwich,' he says. 'Tuna.'

'I don't know.'

'Tuna, so? We'll share it. Order for us,' he says to his daughter. 'Tuna sandwich. No onion. And two teas. Get yourself something. And find us seats. Somewhere quiet.'

He pulls his wife around to the bathroom. Their daughter – what, fourteen, fifteen? – does as she was told. I'll drop it all down to you, the woman at the counter says to her. She's looking around for three seats together, somewhere quiet. They aren't to be had. She sits at the long table, facing me. There are free seats on either side of me. They will have to do for her parents.

She doesn't ask me to move. Her father would hardly expect that of her. You don't say to an older man, one twenty years older than your father: *Do you mind moving please, we are a family and we need to sit together alone.* Maybe she wants a stranger in the mix. Every family has a few bombs ticking. One could blow at a communal table in a small café, splattering innocent onlookers with tea and tuna. Maybe a stranger could cut the fuse for her. But that could cut either way, couldn't it?

She's looking down into her phone. Pale face. Stayed-up-late face. No make-up. Now I can hear you saying it, Elaine: *Cheek of you, Eamon. Mind your own business.* But if you were here you'd say the same. She could do with a touch. I know, they get younger and younger for starting the whole cover-up business and once they start there's no going back, but in her case a smidge of something in the cheeks would not go amiss. She's wearing an over-sized jumper with a hole in the left elbow. Did she look in the mirror at herself this morning and say this will do? This is how I want to step into the world today, I don't care what people think? I don't buy it. I've sat across from my fair share of baggy-eyed teenagers. What people make of them is what keeps them awake. It's when you get to my stage you can let go of all that. You can say and do what you like. Nobody's looking, nobody cares.

Her parents are back. He is still holding on to his wife. Not pulling now, more leading her by the hand to the table. He looks at his daughter's proposed seating arrangement. She gets what I'm willing to venture is his trademark glare.

I move down one seat so he and his wife can sit together.

'Thanks,' he says.

'Not a bother,' I say.

The girl and her parents form a triangle across the table, as if they are interviewing her for a job. What would you be hoping to achieve in the position of our daughter? Do you have any relevant qualifications? Are you willing to relocate if the job requires it? Where do you see yourself in ten years? Her mother has angled her chair away from the table and is staring into the street.

'They're bringing the stuff down,' the daughter says.

'OK. And you said no onion,' her father says.

'I said no onion.'

'And the change?'

She unclenches her fist and lays coins and a receipt on the table. He sweeps it across into his open palm.

'Do I have to ask you every time,' he says. 'Just one time you might offer?'

'You were in the bathroom. What was I supposed to do, slide it under the door?'

He puts his hand up in the *enough* shape. His wife leans into him and says something. I am the wrong side of him to hear it.

'She said they're bringing it down. Just, wait,' he says.

She moves to stand up. He puts his hand on her leg.

'Margaret. They're bringing it down.' It's busy though. Things are not moving as quickly as he wants.

'Watch her,' he says to his daughter as he stands up.

She watches her mother. Margaret puts a leg to the floor and looks out to the street. Her daughter raises her back in the chair, like she's poised to spring if necessary.

'Mam,' she says. 'Mam, he's coming back. He's coming back in a minute.'

He returns with a tray. His daughter leans back in her chair.

'If you need something doing,' he says. He doles out their orders.

'Now. Tuna, no onion. As requested. And your, whatever this is. And the tea.'

He slides a pale orange drink over to his daughter. He removes the lids from the tea and peers in.

'Tea with *milk*. Did you not tell them, one with milk and one without?' he says to his daughter.

'I did. Maybe they're mixed up? Does yours, have—?'

He sing-songs his answer in an exasperated voice. 'Yes, *Lauren*. Mine *has* milk. I *take* milk. Your mother does *not*. Mine is *right*. Hers is *wrong*.'

'I'll go up,' Lauren says.

'I'll have it with milk, it's fine,' Margaret says.

'Since when is that *fine*,' her husband says. 'You don't take milk. Why would you start now?'

Lauren rises and takes the wrong tea back to the counter. Margaret looks to the street again, then looks down. Her husband drinks from the right tea. This couple are perched on their stools, both looking down at the floor. They look like a folk duo with no songs left in their set and nobody calling for an encore.

'So. Did you enjoy the walk?' he says to Margaret.

'What?'

'The walk. Did you enjoy it?'

'Yes. Just now?'

'Yes just now. What do you mean?'

'We went along the Dodder, just now.'

'Yes Margaret. We went along the Dodder just now, then it started raining and we came in here.'

'I know we did. That's what I'm saying. I'm not, what do you think?'

'I don't think anything.'

They turn away from each other, looking forward at our shared table.

'You're upsetting the day,' Margaret says to her husband.

'Upsetting, what?' he says.

'Where's Lauren?' she asks.

'She's right there. Look,' he says, pointing to Lauren, who is coming back from the counter.

'One tea, no *milk*,' Lauren says, placing it in front of her mother.

'Thank you, *Lauren*,' her father says.

He picks up the cup, removes the lid and fishes out the bag with a stick, and replaces the lid. He holds the cup out for his wife to take. She puts her hands around it.

'Now,' he says. 'We are all fine.'

Lauren puts her earphones in and picks up her drink. Her head dips down into her phone again. Margaret picks up her half of the sandwich and takes a tentative, birdlike bite.

'How's your ... what is that,' Lauren's father says to her.

She takes her earphones out. 'What?'

'What is that.'

'Peach iced tea.'

'*Peach iced tea.* How is it.'

'Fine, yeah.'

'And your sandwich?' he says to Margaret.

'It's fine,' she says.

'Least we haven't lost the art of conversation,' he says to the air. Or it might have half been to me. I keep my eyes on the newspaper. I'm not about to get into the ring.

He picks up his half of the sandwich and takes a bite. He stops and prises it open. He lifts it up to his eyes and examines it like a watchmaker.

'Is there onion in this? There is. Jesus *Christ*, Lauren.'

He flings the sandwich onto the table.

'Frank,' Margaret says.

'What is so difficult about ...' Frank is saying in the direction of the sandwich.

'Frank,' she says again. 'What is this?'

'It's a tuna sandwich that someone *allegedly* said not to put onion in,' Frank says, looking at Lauren. 'But nobody listens, do they?'

'I told them,' Lauren says. 'I did, Dad.'

She did. I heard her. I could say so. In fairness, Frank, she did. But then I'm a witness for the defence and there could be all sorts of follow-on questions. Your honour, who the hell is this old man listening in to our private conversation? Kindly leave us be.

Frank grips the edge of the table. Perhaps one of those bombs is about to go off. Because of the problems with the sandwich and the tea and the day in general. Maybe he'll stand up on his chair and shout *what kind of circus is this? All we wanted was what we asked for. You are the ones upsetting the day.*

'What is this?' Margaret asks again, holding her cup out in front of her.

'It's ... it's your tea, Margaret,' Frank says.

'Yes.'

'Just drink it,' he says.

She holds it up to her lips, her eyes on him. He is staring down at the table and does not see the look she gives him. I see it and I've seen it. *Is this what you do? You hold it up to your lips? And drink, like this? Am I doing it the way you want me to? Am I doing it right?*

Margaret lets her tea fall to the floor. It is not knocked from her hands. It is not an accident. I saw it. She just let it go. Frank jumps up from his chair. Margaret looks down at the tawny wave lapping around their feet. I try to look away. But we're all close together. It is under my chair, Frank, I'm in it too. Before you accuse me of sticking my snout in.

'You're alright,' Frank says, standing up and pushing his chair back. 'You're alright.'

'What happened?' Lauren asks, taking out her earphones again.

'It's OK,' says Frank. 'It's OK. It was an accident.'

'I need to go,' Margaret says, looking down at the stain on her skirt.

'I'll bring you to the bathroom. You didn't get much on yourself, it's alright,' he says.

'I'll bring her, Dad,' Lauren says, standing too.

Margaret looks at the ground, then at her family. 'I need to go,' she says again. And with a deftness I didn't expect to see in her, she springs to her feet and walks out the door into the street and the rain. She moves like a child: lurching forward, head down and heedless.

'Watch our stuff,' Lauren's father says to her, and he goes after his wife, leaving his daughter and a spreading mess for someone else to attend to.

It's been five minutes since they made for the door. Lauren is holding down what's left of the fort. She's cast a look up at the door a few times, then sunk back into her phone, a pale sheen on her face from its light. What is she telling herself? *We are fine. This is fine.*

These young people, they want you to think they're well able. They slouched in front of me year after year, doing a confidence trick on themselves. The two gifts of youth: to have no clue, and to not yet know it. *I can handle whatever you throw at me, boss*. Each unaware how the world will grab them by the throat and say *can you now, musha*. Not all of them, to be fair. Maybe not Lauren. She reminds me of another young girl who learned to cop on quick. She stood up just now, looked to the door and sat back down again. *What should I do*, she must be wondering. I'm asking myself the same. Other people's problems are just that. Tend to my own and leave them be. That would be my wife's instruction. Her name is Elaine and I am Eamon, her husband. I tell her this every day. Reset the record with each visit. No, I am not your Uncle Brendan. I am Eamon, your husband. Yes, I did visit you yesterday. I wrote my name in the book by your bed and put the date on it. So there wouldn't be any confusion. So don't be making up stories that you haven't seen me in months. I am here every day and I am Eamon, your husband. She's not here now though. I know what I shouldn't do, and I do it anyway. The only gift of old age: do what you want.

I tap Lauren on the arm and she looks up.

'Did you want to go out after them? I will watch your stuff,' I say.

'No, I'm fine, thank you.'

No you're not Lauren. Sorry Elaine, but if you could see her here. It's like when you got sunburn that day. Everyone else could see you were on fire except you.

'Not a fan of the Mexican chicken?' I say.

'Sorry?'

'Your sandwich there.'

She's left it untouched since it arrived. The woman who brought it over is mopping the floor under us. The accident never happened, according to the floor at least.

'I don't know what they're about with the Mexican. Has a bit of salsa and a few Doritos on the side, sure, but it's not exactly Acapulco on a plate,' I say. I've had every sandwich in here and I nearly warned her off the Mexican but let the young ones make their own mistakes.

She looks down at it. 'Yeah it's not great.'

'I'm sure they'll be back soon, don't be worrying,' I say.

'Yep, they're just getting some air.'

'Well. Can't beat a bit of air.'

'They'll be back in a minute,' she says.

She reaches down to her bag and takes out a book. *The Past Today.* She must seriously want to be left alone to resort to a schoolbook. I hear you, Lauren. *Back off. I can take care of myself.* I hear you too, Elaine. *Nobody wants your study tips. They don't teach it like that anymore.* But now we're on my specialist subject.

'Junior Cert this year?'

'Yep.'

'Hitting the books.'

'Well, trying to.'

Grubby old copy of it, second- or third-hand. She has a highlighter out. Going over someone else's faded yellow with a fresh coat. Taking for granted its previous owner knew what was worth knowing. As they probably did before her. One overkeen paint-slinger leading subsequent generations down the primrose path. Look at her getting on with it. Earphones back in. Leave her be.

I could tell her about the past today. I could tell her about the future too. You taught me that, Elaine. And I didn't walk away from you in the shops. Stop saying that. We agreed where and when to meet. Outside

Coffee for 2 at two o'clock. I made it easy to remember. *Coffee for 2 at two, darling.* I thought about tracking you around the shops, hanging back, make sure you were OK. But I didn't want to insult you. I was there at two. Where were you? I had turned up the ring-tone on your phone but you weren't answering. I called our daughter.

'Aisling. Has your mother stopped in by any chance?'

'No. Why?'

'OK, no she's just ...'

'Is she not with you?'

'She's probably just in a shop and has no signal. Not to worry.'

'Dad, where are you?'

'In Dundrum. We said we'd meet at two.'

'Do you want me to come down?'

'Don't be silly, it's fine. I'm sure she'll be here in a minute.'

'I'll try and call her.'

'OK yes, you try too, Aisling. Don't be worrying.'

Let's all try and reach you. Let's all stop worrying. I called the home phone. But why would you be there? I couldn't see you making your own way home. Not at that stage. The Luas has too many steps, we agreed. You wouldn't have tried that alone, would you? Maybe you got a taxi. But you would have told me. Wouldn't you? I called the neighbours. *No Eamon, she's not with us.* They knew. They knew as well as I did. Will we come down? No it's fine. I wanted to keep things to ourselves, but time was passing and there was no sign and no choice. I had to announce it to the world. I had them call your name out. *Would Elaine McGovern please come to the help desk on level one where her husband is waiting, thank you.* I could barely hear it myself over the racket in there. What chance had you?

'It's not even quarter past, I wouldn't be worrying,' the security guard said to me.

'It's not even Christmas yet, I wouldn't be worrying,' I say to Lauren.

She looks up from her book. Yes. I'm still here. Tenacious old bollix.

'Have the mocks though.'

'Ah, the mocks. Sure they're just a bit of a frightener. All my students failed them every year. They did grand on the day.'

'Are you a teacher?'

'I was. Retired now.'

'What did you teach?'

'History, mainly,' I say, tapping her book. 'Where are you up to in there?'

'The civil war.'

'Which one?'

'There's more than one?'

Ah, Lauren. Wait until I get up to Elaine and tell her that one.

'There've been a few now, yeah.'

'I'm not good at history,' she says.

'I'm sure you're better than you think.'

'I'm not. I just don't, get the point, really.'

'The point of ... history?'

'Yeah. I mean. It's over. So ...?' She shrugs off the Famine, whichever civil war and all the rest of it in one gesture.

It's fair enough though. I've heard it before. Why bother, sir? Everyone in it is dead, sir. So we can learn from the past, I used to say. Which got the groans it deserved. Because it's a good story. I tried that line for a while, but if anything that's more of a lie. Stories are supposed to add up to something. History is just one thing after another. Nobody learns a thing from it. But I should honour the fallen soldiers lying dead in her neon yellow field with some words.

'Do a bit of revision here so. I won't bother you. But whatever civil war it is, I'll tell you this much: brother rose up against brother and people died for no good reason.'

Sit back with that, and do what I promised. Don't bother her. I could give myself some study tips too. Don't take on so many subjects, for a start. Widen a circle of concern across communal tables and out into the world, end up taking in drunks off the street and asking them if they need to call someone. If you are going to live calmly, sanely, well in yourself, you need to say to nearly all in view: I see your trouble, and I'm sorry for it, but I am not about to wade into your dark waters. That's how you get through the test.

But some people can't be left to float alone. Put a ring around one other and promise: we sail or sink together. When you called I was fit to take your head off.

'Where in the name of God are you, Elaine? It's nearly three?'

'Hello, is that Eamon?' A man's voice.

'Who is this?'

'My name's Peter Whelan. Eamon, Elaine is here with us. I thought you might want to come and ... get her.'

'Come and get her where? Where is she?'

'24 Clonard Road.'

'She took a taxi home, no panic,' I said to Aisling on the phone as I drove there. I didn't tell her which home. Back to the first house we lived in. The one we were sixteen years gone from.

'I'm sorry. I'm sorry about this,' I said to Peter, at our old front door.

'Nothing to be sorry about,' Peter said, inviting me in. Standing there in our old hall was like a strange dream. Who were these people and why were the walls yellow now? What must it have done to you? 'She's in here with my wife Sheila. She's grand now. Just a bit ...'

'She's, it's just ...'

He put up a hand. 'It's no bother at all. Come on through. I think you know the way.'

You were sitting at the kitchen table with this man's wife. Drinking tea as if the world was absolutely as it should be.

'Eamon, look what they've done to our house,' you said. You started moving around the kitchen – their kitchen – like an estate agent. Opening their presses and closing them again. 'You really have made a balls of the place,' you said to its occupants.

Peter roared laughing. 'Not your style now, Elaine?'

He was being nice about it. He was letting you.

'Elaine, we really shouldn't be—'

'Don't worry at all,' Sheila said to me. 'You just wanted to have a look at the old place, Elaine. Sure I'd want to do the same.'

I looked at the countertop. The dents of our tenure erased. The crack from a hot pot one Saturday. My fault. I should have put something under it, you were right. We had a big old row about it. It was gone now, counter and crack, and what did it matter in the end. In the long run we are all ancient history and nobody cares who started which war.

'We used to sit out and look at the planes going over,' you said, looking out into the garden. 'We used to sit and count them. We'd say, let's wait until ten go over. Then we'd go inside. It was a nice way of marking out the time, wasn't it Eamon?'

'It was,' I said. It was.

'Wonder where they're off to, you used to say to me. Boston or Borneo. Cape Town or California. Would you swap with them, you always asked me. And I always said—'

'You said, I'm happy where I am.'

'Would you like to sit out in the garden, Elaine?' Sheila asked. 'We could have our tea out there. Not a bad old day. I mean, stay for dinner? Why not?'

'We will not, Sheila. We're not *swingers*,' you said, in a stage whisper. 'In case you're getting an idea about something. We're not like the McLoughlins and the O'Malleys. Pampas grass in the garden. Wink wink.'

Peter opened his eyes wide to this. What were you at? But I loved hearing you like this again. Keep on swinging.

'Pampas grass. *Oh*. Well that's the giveaway,' Peter said.

'No, having it off with your neighbour is the give-away, Peter,' you said.

That set the lot of us off. You were being trademark outrageous. Here you were again.

'Now stop,' I said. 'Do not be making up stories.'

'What stories? I'm only saying what you used to say. Helen O'Malley hitching her leg over the wall into the neighbours at half eight in the morning in her dressing gown. Riddle me that.'

'Maybe she was out of milk,' Sheila said. She had the sense of the thing. Letting you run on.

'She didn't take *milk*, Sheila,' you said.

'Well, I'd say she did next door,' said Peter. Fair dues to him. He pulled the ring out of the grenade and threw it on the awful fake quartz countertop. You were right. The kitchen was a disgrace. And you were the one laughing the loudest. I didn't think you had any more of those left in your lungs. We were laughing immortal there, in the house you never wanted to leave, divilment long dormant rising up in you again. The way you were with these strangers, like we had invited them over and we were showing how mad we were, and this was nothing but a slip-up, a funny little episode. You went on auto-pilot back to your old house, could happen to anyone, and we were fine. Everything was absolutely as it should be.

You stopped yourself laughing with a hand to your mouth.

'Shhh,' you said to us all. 'We'll wake Aisling.'

That was our first full day in the new weather, Lauren. Is today yours? Or maybe you're well worn into it. It's hard to see it coming. One minute it's not raining. Then you feel a drop land on your arm. Deny it all you want. The rain has no regard for your wishes. She's old enough to know this. I tap the page of her book, to get her attention again. If that's not too much of an intrusion. I don't care if it is. Privacy be damned, Elaine.

'Can I give you some study advice?' I say.

'Uh, sure.'

'Let me write out some key points for you. Some things to keep in mind. Tear off a page of your copybook there.'

'I probably, shouldn't ...'

'I know. You shouldn't talk to strangers. I'm not, like that, Lauren. I want to help you. Just let an old crow of a teacher be helpful.'

She tears out a page for me. I write a few notes to her. Fight for Independence, Civil War, rise of the Free State. And a few pointers to bring her up to the present. I hand it to her.

'And can I give you a bit more advice. Not about, all this,' I say, waving a hand over her book.

'About what?'

'About, you know. Your mother.'

Her eyes widen. Have I lit a fuse now, Lauren? Will we keep her lit?

'Mam,' she says.

But she's looking over my shoulder. Her parents have come back in the door. Soaked again. Back where they started.

'All fine,' Frank says to her. He's sitting back down on his chair. Helping Margaret back onto hers.

'Are you OK, Mam?' Lauren asks.

'Your mother was just feeling a bit hot so we took a little walk and sat down for a while. We're fine now.'

'Mam?' Lauren asks again.

'Yes. I was just a little hot,' she says.

I should say something. Before Lauren does.

'Excuse me, sorry, but I have just been talking to Lauren here,' I say to Frank. 'And I wanted to compliment you on raising such a polite and pleasant young lady.'

He looks at me. Lauren is reddening. Nothing more horrific than complimenting a young person in front of them. Even with all of their stuff about likes. Like my picture. Look at how many likes it got. They don't want to hear it to their face.

'Thank you,' he says. Though his face says *talking to her about what.*

'It isn't easy for them. With all the things that come at them,' I say.

'It isn't, no,' he says.

'And I'm sorry now for overhearing but these nits put onion in your sandwich, even though Lauren did tell them not to. I heard her myself,' I say to Margaret, talking a little louder. I want her to hear me clearly.

'I don't like the texture,' she says, looking at her husband to confirm that's right, isn't it. I don't like the texture and *who is this.*

'That's right,' Frank says. 'You don't.'

'I spilled my tea. Hope we didn't . . . get you,' Margaret says to me.

Frank puts a hand on her arm. 'We don't need to go back into that. It was an accident. We are OK now.'

'Sure those paper cups are treacherous. And no little cardboard thing around it,' I say. 'All cleaned up now anyway. Gave us a bit of excitement.'

She laughs. 'Excitement. Now we all need a bit of that.'

'You're not wrong there,' I say.

Frank looks at her. Then at me. *Why are you talking to us? Why, Margaret, are you talking to him? If we stay completely still will you stay like this?*

I don't know how it works, Frank. All I know is we have to keep talking. We have to keep them on the line. If we stop, the silence will soak into us all.

'I think we'll make a move,' he says to her, turning away from me.

'I think I want another tea,' Margaret says.

'Another one. After ... alright, so.'

Good man, Frank. Let her have what she wants, while she can still have a want. He stands up and looks down at this old crone talking to his wife. *What are you at? Are you to be trusted? What might go down if I leave you in charge?* Don't worry Captain. I'll steer clear of the rocks. He goes up to the counter.

'Think I hear a touch of the West,' I say to Margaret.

'You do indeed. Louisburgh. Up Mayo.'

'Two of us in it,' I say. 'I'm from Bohola.'

'There's three pubs in Bohola. Do you know that song?' she says.

'I do of course,' I say. Maybe I've got her wrong. Maybe she's miles and years away yet. Maybe she just spilled her tea and wanted some air, can happen to anyone.

'I go swimming in Carrownisky,' she says.

'Brave woman. Dangerous enough if you don't know what you're doing. Fierce riptides there.'

'I am a good swimmer.'

'My wife used to swim there too.'

'Is she dead?'

'Mam,' says Lauren.

I see where she is. That's not how we say it, Margaret. I would say she has not been in the sea many's the year.

'We might get down to Carrownisky later,' she says to her daughter. 'Would you like that, Lauren? Quick dip?'

'Eh, let's see, Mam.'

Go on Lauren. Humour her. It's only a four-hour drive to Carrownisky, on a blackening Sunday at the sharp end of November. Lauren is looking away from me. Margaret has sat back in her chair and her eyes are closing. Where is she now? Back in the frozen sea, pulling herself up, saying I'm here, I'm still here. Riptide, how are yeh? I'll swim right through you and dare you to drag me down.

Frank is back and in between us. He puts the tea on the table.

'Just let me know when you want a sip,' he says.

'She's full of chat,' I say to him. He looks at me and something narrows and darkens. I've said it too low to him. She is not my patient. She is not in my classroom. Done it again, haven't I, Elaine? Mind my own. I don't listen.

'Why wouldn't she be?' Frank says, staring into me. I know that face. It was mine a good while.

'No reason at all,' I say. 'I was just ...'

'I think we'll just ... if you don't mind,' he says, and he turns his back on me.

Ah Frank. You don't have to look at me that way. It's the same look I gave to Barry, in the hall of our old house as we left. We're fine, I said to Barry, answering the question he didn't ask. That's what you say when strangers push on the door. It's what Lauren said. It's what Frank will say if I push any further. I know what you're thinking, Frank, same as I've thought, looking into the mirror and at her: I am terrified. Dark and selfish thoughts will come too. Will I catch it from her? Is it soaking through my cells? Did we breathe in something in a town in Italy and it's in our lungs and she's telling my future? Will our own daughter be feeding us at her kitchen table like a pair of dribbling grey twins? That's all coming up and at you. The tide comes in and the rain comes down and only a lunatic would take up arms against them. And only an idiot wouldn't take a hand into the lifeboat. Never mind what promises were made. Sink with the ship and nobody's saved. Listen to some good advice. Don't leave it like this. I won't.

'I just meant,' I say to his back. 'I just, my wife – we went through, I know what it's like.'

He turns around to me. 'My wife is fine, thank you very much,' he says.

Why are we like this? We're fortresses under siege, boiling oil raining down on us, but when someone tries to open the drawbridge, what do we say? I'm fine thanks. We're OK. Does anyone here have a clue?

'Lauren,' I say. 'Wasn't I helping you with your studies?'

'Yes, thanks.'

'I can tell you're a good student. She's doing alright, Frank.'

'Yes, she is. Are you alright, though?' he says.

'Sorry?' Why would I not be?

'Just, you were, talking to yourself there. Singing some song about Bohola. Saying something about boiling oil. Are you alright?'

'I'll leave you be,' I say.

Elaine, the absolute cheek of him? Going in on me like that. Covering up for his wife. Making me out like the cuckoo after all their carrying on. After me helping Lauren with her studies and me talking to his wife better than he could. He was jealous, was that it? Doesn't have the right way with either of them. Hold it in, say nothing. The state you're in, son. What you're doing to poor Lauren. After all the help I had to give. I will not sit and be insulted. I'm out the door and well away from them now. And I wasn't singing. But I'll sing if I want. If there's a tune in my head and I can carry it well enough what's wrong with that? There's not enough people singing, Frank, that's the problem. Do you not know how to be to people? I'll tell you. Same as Elaine told Aisling and me. Sitting in our back garden one day when we were taking in the last of the sun, little burn on her cheeks, after things had started to sink, after months of *can you make a cup of tea, show me, no look, it's kettle on first*, then quietly taking over that and everything. You just wait, Frank. Wait until you're holding the woman who used to push you down on the bed, you wait until you're holding her on the toilet seat. That's all ahead. Like it was ahead of me then. Elaine had one of those wild moments where she swam to the surface, and saw us, and grabbed a mouthful of air. Aisling saw it in her.

'What is it, Mam?' she said.

Elaine leaned over to her, put a hand on Aisling's chest and said: *Leave me be.* She held her hand there like she was pushing it in. Then she turned to me and said it again. And then she sat back and sank back, her instructions embedded in us. Now, *I love you*: any fool can say that, and hope to hear an echo. *Leave me be*, though. That is a different class of an ask altogether. Could you manage it, Frank? How about yourself, Lauren? If Margaret says *Leave me, be.* Live your life and don't lose yourself. Don't make me the reason you did not. I hope you're both ready for that, when it comes.

'Go on Aisling,' I said, when the first test came. 'Go on. I want you to.'

'I don't want to leave you alone.'

'You're not leaving me alone. There's two of us aboard yet.'

'You know what I mean.'

'And what are you going to do? Sit here and wait? Would you get out there and take over the world, please. The state it's in, someone has to. And that visa will expire if you don't use it.'

'I'd be back in a second, if there's …'

'I know you would. Sure it's only a six-hour flight. Take longer if you were in Dingle.'

She had already decided, of course. Gang of them heading off. Why wouldn't she? I would have, if I was her. Lauren, you'll feel this, the pull of the world on you. There's no meanness in it. You'll do what Aisling did, if you've any sense. She heard what the boss said.

She calls when she can. Called last night, in fact. Was it last night? I think it was.

'I've a new job, Dad.'

'Oh that's great, Aisling. Who's that with now?'

'You wouldn't know the name. They're one of the big agencies out here.'

'Oh very good. And what is the job?'

'Brand communications director.'

I couldn't hear her very well. It sounded like she's on a train. There's a twang come into her voice, the words going up like balloons at the end of each sentence.

'I read a story in the paper about a flood in Ontario,' I said.

'Yeah. That was miles from here.'

'Alright. Just, you know how to handle yourself in that situation. You go to the higher ground.'

'OK. Dad, are you OK?'

'Why wouldn't I be?'

★

I send her letters. I'm no good with the computer. I tell her about the people I meet. I'll write to her about Lauren. I met a girl who reminded me of you when you were fifteen, Aisling. I gave her some study tips, like I used to give you. Lauren might put my tips in the bin. Or she might show them to her Dad. She might be doing that right now and he's coming up the road after me. But I expect she'll just stick them in her book and forget. Maybe she'll find them on a hot June evening when she's left it too late and cramming it in. It's just some advice for what's coming up, a teacher's tip for the test: *When the time comes, leave her be and live your life.* If I'm going to stick into other people's business, at least I'll stick in something useful. Rip it up, look away, makes no odds to me. I've said my bit.

I'll be up to you soon Elaine. I'm well up the road now. I should not leave it so long. I'll tell you all about Lauren too. She really did remind me of our Aisling. She's coming home in a few weeks. She wants to visit and bring flowers. I told her on the phone, was it last week, don't you remember your mother's allergic to pollen? Don't you remember that? She worries about me on my own. Are you OK, she keeps saying, do you need any help, should I call someone. I keep telling her: I'm fine. Don't be worrying. Leave me be. Don't you remember what we all agreed?

WONDERHOUSE (SOME ASSEMBLY REQUIRED)

Thank you on purchase of Eager Minds WonderHouse™! We hope it will bring you and your little explorers many hours of wonder and fun in years to come. Please follow these instructions <u>carefully</u> to ensure safe and pleasant use.

Step 1: Check you have all parts listed below.
Parts missing? Please call helpline number shown on page 28.

28 pages. Check to see if some are in German/ Chinese/etc. and can be skipped. Are not. Skip to page 28 to imagine/spoil ending. Sketch of triumphantly assembled structure with stick figure man, hand on hip, arm extended over creation, ready to commence many hours of fun and wonder complete with squeals of gratitude from daughter or similar loved one (not pictured).

Turn from glorious outcome back to Step 1 reality. All parts checked and present. Parts many and various but trust all necessary and purpose will be revealed in due course. Separate into ordered alphabetised piles on carpet. Not all letters used. Be grateful 9 piles not 26 though. Create adequate space along with surely adequate 2 hours on Saturday afternoon. Now 4 p.m. To be assembled by 6 p.m. and delivered to D for 7 p.m. Fun/wonder commences 7.15 p.m. Picture this: Oh wow this is the best thing ever etc. Oh no trouble no took less time than

I thought you're very welcome etc. Picture this and press on.

Step 2: *Have you all necessary tools? For this you will also need:*

1 Phillips head screwdriver
1 hammer
2 people to support weight (NOTE: it is to assemble alone unsafe).

Check. Check. Not check. Just one person. Surely multitudes optional? One person (Part Y, You) was well able to drag box in here on own. Can't be heavier coming out. Have basic grasp of physics thanks. Cannot increase mass. Can only apply force and energy. So easily pulled in wrong distracting direction. Focus now.

Weird word order too, re *assemble alone unsafe*. Awkward translation from the original? Ominous/ poetic tone is mildly disquieting. Also note step has defined people as tools.

Tools also present and necessary:

1 'Ambient Relaxation' playlist (to put mind in calm receptive place during assembly)

1 Galway Hooker IPA 50cl 4.8% (for similar reasons.1 only as timely delivery top priority and assembly-transport-presentation arduous enough without additional snags).

Note 26 minutes gone and so far have just arranged various screws and planks in pleasing but passive manner on carpet.

Step 3: *Locate Planks A. Insert short head Screws J into Planks A at intervals (see Fig. 2). Be sure to insert screws into <u>upper side</u>.*

Planks A located and upsided. Very compliant. Screws more inscrutable. Piles of unmarked screws of various dimensions. J = ? Does short head mean shortest screw? Or smallest head? Or only screws that will fit holes in Planks A? Or all of these? Try a few screws. Most fit quite nicely into Planks A. Cinderella moment this is not. But do not force. Know from experience that complexities arise if incorrect parts forced into wrong fittings. Realise J was marked on one of many small plastic packages, but in haste to comply with Step 1 Y removed all screws from packages and now no way to say which sprang from J-pack. This is what happens when instructions not followed. Pleasant-looking piles now swirling screwniverse of chaos. Enter realm of damned at 4.42 p.m. Open beer (1).

Unsurrender. Count holes in Planks A. 24. Count number of screws in each pile. Only 1 of 24 identicals. Pride self on deductive abilities. Kneel to urge ranks of J into planks of A. Some Js do not insert very neatly. Some gone in at quite an angle. Attempt to restore order but screwdriver is scratching and tearing at J heads. Partial misalignment = end of world? Surely slightly loose connection won't cause WonderHouse to collapse trapping/severely injuring occupants. Think of engineers whose similar nonchalant approach caused derailments, infernos, years of inquests. Overthinking. Future joy will not be structurally compromised by a few rogue elements.

Steps 1 to 3 have consumed 48 minutes of allotted 120. Maybe disproportionately onerous? 4 to 27 possibly accelerated path to glory? Regard again page 28. Note how stick face smile imparts pride, relief, excellent parenting. Aspire towards. Open beer (2). Doesn't count, as sweating it out anyway? Can always get taxi, might actually be better plan? Transport easier in a people carrier? Restart playlist as was not in calm receptive mood during Step 3 and milky piano floaty voices swishing wavy noises did not have intended effect.

Step 4: Simply place Planks A onto Base B as shown, taking care to align screws with holes in base. Do not force.
Not simply. B rejects any suggestion of alignment with A. Bear mild to medium resentment towards breezy nature in which step is described, belying feat of human endeavour within. *Simply place Space Shuttle into Earth's Atmosphere as shown, taking care to align with landing site.* Do not explode. *Simply place Flag onto Omaha Beach as shown, taking care to overwhelm enemy forces.* Do not get massacred. Some force clearly necessary. Align Planks A inelegantly/ quite violently onto B. Cracking noise registered but no sign of exterior damage.

Stand up slowly, allowing flow of O positive to return to compromised legs of Y. Push against teetering Base B with beer empty (2). Go to kitchen and find remedy for unsteadiness. Assemble auxiliary screwdriver, carefully aligning Smirnoff, orange juice and ice. Liberally apply thoughts of other parts Y has forced into position but came unstuck. Specifically:

C: Celina, in Y's life and house and so welcome until *I am sorry but we cannot be anymore.*

D: Deana, Celina's daughter and your wonder but *not your daughter is not yours understand this please.*

E: Elek, previously concealed component *his daughter his understand this and yes still my husband by law and coming here arriving I did not know believe me but he wants.*

Place Parts C and D on top of screwdriver and beer (3). Recall attempts to combine Y, C and D. All held together well enough at first and did not force, but Y did not see missing part. E was not referred to in initial assembly, an oversight which is *sorry I am sorry wanted to tell you many times and could not but now he is and we must please.*

E cleared customs and has been delivered. E now recombined with C and D per original design, completing unit. Temporary Part Y no longer required. Can now be removed/discarded. Y was briefly load bearing and *thankful yes grateful but understand this is how we must be.* CDE now free-standing unit functioning as intended *do not call.* If desired, or not, Y can be left in current position at right angle to WonderHouse, which at present work rate seems unlikely to be successfully delivered to intended and unsuspecting recipient. D not permanently connected to Y as was *clearly documented.* D's wonder is *not your concern anymore.* Delivery to D is very much at Y's own risk. Manufacturer cannot be held responsible for consequences if WonderHouse used for unintended purposes.

Step 5: Now insert Hex Head Screws H into Base B in indicated holes (see Fig. 3).

Prowl around B menacingly with screwdrivers (1 of each). No holes indicated. Fall to knees and align eyes with plywood. Tilt Base B upwards from carpet to examine. In looking upwards regard mantlepiece and pic of Y that D drew. Observe space next to fireplace where box of D's dolls/toys were previously in position. Colour of wallpaper unfaded in unoccupied space glaring at Y.

Turn back to Base B to note that indicated holes are on underside. Fig. 3 shows they should be opposite of underside. Stare at row of pre-cut holes. Three dots in inverted triangles, each two eyes with open mouth saying *oh, oh, oh, are you surprised? That's your problem. If you ask us Y should have looked ahead maybe seen what was coming?* Now staring into the plywood face of all effort wasted. Somewhat uncarefully turn Base upside down. In doing so, observe how Planks A swiftly untether themselves from their *at best temporary arrangement* with B. Consider fading light and disconnected WonderParts in floor pile at 6.28 p.m. Help needed. Helpline closes 5 p.m. Saturdays. Unhelpful.

Stand up. Take measure of enemy. Take steps necessary.

Rip page 28 from instructions and set aside.
Compress rest of commands into ball and apply to wall with fully justified force. Prepare screwdriver (3), adjusting ratio of V to OJ as required, tilting head to required angle. Remove shirt to regulate internal temperature. Kill 'Forest Rain' sounds. Switch to 'Power Workout' playlist.

Unleash hell on Wonder.
Let anger, tools, beers, screws become one. Enter zone spoken of by top-performing athletes and musicians. This just wood from a tree and screws from a factory. This is not the undoing of Y this is just an obstacle life consists of these. Can cower in corner or push into them over them conquer them. Can be making of a person. Can look back and think was that really so overwhelming and anyway what kind of person surrenders just lies down says you win. No no no. Let these thoughts guide hands now.

At 7.34 p.m. step back and consider WonderStructure, supported by interior actual wall to which it is now affixed, filling space where D's toys and D used to be. Side panels looking as if have weathered sitting room Category

4 storm, several crooked and cracked. Decorative Fencing F doing additional job of partially holding door in place. Roof slanting off sharply to left. Overall look is less WonderHouse more WitchHovel. WonderHouse now permanently inside your house. Not going anywhere. Assume stick man pose and cast arm over. Say look what you made, to assembled mass and nobody. You think I'm good for nothing? Well there was nothing here and now there is this and isn't that something?

Not yet it isn't. Parts missing. Parts that were holding Y up. Need to call.

Call helpline.
Text pic of WonderHouse (box not actual) to C. Call C. Explain to C that Y needs to connect with D, now, yes now. C refuses. Reapply with a little more force, taking care not to break tenuous connection. Give me this. Today give me this.

Allow sufficient time for words to dry in air. Adding further words on top of first layer too quickly may cause cracking of C. *Please, you cannot. I will let this just today but then no more please understand you cannot.*

D is connected. Tell her Y has a great surprise for her. Tell D to look at pic just sent and say surprise happy birthday look what I made for you. Do you want to come over and see it? Why not today why not right now? No, Y can't bring it to D's new house. Silly Y. I built your Wonder inside mine and now it's stuck. Need you here. Come over today? Would love to see you again, darling. Y missing parts so called helpline. *I'm not allowed,* D says.

D disconnects. C returns to call. Tone appears darker than previous. If Y persists, C advises that an application of E may be required to remove unwanted stain. E can be dispatched at very short notice. *I'm warning you. Please stop. For I do not know. What he will do.*

Deal with snag list.

Work on into darkness. Might have visitors one/several any minute. Address snags. Main one being E. Can deal with E though. Said so on phone when he connected. Come on over big man. Dealt with worse. Can't be harder to force into position than planks/screws. As fixing WonderDoor (swinging loosely off hinges) picture E coming to actual house door. E would be free-standing powerfully built unit. Would invite E in. Well Elek, I wondered when we'd have a little chat. Would hold beer (6) behind back. Would extend arm over WonderHouse. Say to him, what do you think? Care to step inside? Then with screwed up face and bottle give him instructions clearly: You think you can just, out of nowhere? And turn my life upside down? Miss them still love them you weren't here you can't just, though these words loosely balanced and slipping off screwdriver/beer base.

Enter WonderHouse.

Easier to work on snags from inside. Lift door off as if inhuman strength which some people get in moment when fully necessary. Actually hanging by one screw not difficult. Crawl in on knees. Turn slowly onto back, bring head up, eyeballing screws jutting out at Y pointing mocking *what are you doing in here? Do you know what you're doing?* Bash screws with beer empty (7). Picture bashing empty against E with force fully necessary. One good swing fixing him permanently in place, fixing situation for good. Text C. I have rights too this is your final warning please. Send. Tight in here but also snug hideaway. Some houses just too big and empty. This one inside Y's is full with people, person, one. Could take two. Picture as if camping in a forest, gentle rain falling, warm yellow glow, safe in here. Could hang fairy lights as through loose panel in back can reach plug in house wall. Build a good feeling. Keep it together. D, we could be something in here. But wouldn't hold her. Picture D growing like sped-up nature video pushing Y aside bursting through roof climbing out and looking back at Y *oh, oh, oh did you think you could keep me in there? I'm off to Poznan with my actual Dad, you tool.* Please. Please let me. Text unread. Knocking, who, how, there's no door? Come in D I'm here come back C I forgive you let's go E I'm ready breathe stand up get—

Leave to dry for at least 12 hours.
A thin layer of O positive now coating WonderHouse yellow plastic floor. Gauge quality of morning light coming in through now open-plan WonderRoof via real house window.

Recall final steps from previous evening.

Heard knocking on exterior door. Almost certain heard knocking. Rose to deal with/welcome/forgive depending on delivery. However was in compromised position inside WonderHouse long into night and internal balance/awareness of surroundings not functioning correctly. Cracked head through roof. Looked into darkness before falling backwards aligning with several exposed J and H screws on Base B.

Y in Y shape now, legs extended 45 degrees in opposite directions through where windows should be. Roof Plate now red plastic blanket on chest. Fixed/screwed in DeadWitch position.

Should exit WonderHouse now. Seized. Condemned. Due for demolition. Remain instead in void while joints resettle. Could call helpline. Reach out to page 28 on floor in O positive pool. But aware now that warranty is voided. Helpline closed. Text unread.

Uncrumple page 28. Look in pale morning upon stick man, stick arm forever stretching towards impossible, stick face grimace fixed in everlasting anticipation of many unwondrous years to come.

TOOTH AND BONE

BEN SHOULD NOT WORRY SO much. His Dad and sister told him so when they were out for dinner. You are a worrier, his Dad said. Life is short. Try and enjoy it. You're setting my teeth on edge, his sister Mia said.

Ben ran his tongue over his back teeth. Some of them were sharp but they were the right side up. One of them was hurting, at the back, on the right. A throb. He had told his Dad. It wasn't like a take me to the dentist right away I can't stand it throb. It was saying I'm here and it's not right, and I'm not going away. But don't make a fuss about me now. Don't start worrying. Wait until it gets worse.

'If you're going to worry, worry big,' Ben's Dad said to him, looking at the menu. 'Don't worry about small things like a sore tooth. There's a war going on. An actual war. People are being bombed and shot at.'

'Where is the war?' Ben asked him.

'Thousands of miles away. So don't worry about it. I'm just saying there are big things.'

'If you fight in a war it's OK to shoot people,' Ben said. 'You don't get in trouble.'

'That's right. That's what they want you to do.'

'What if you say no, I don't want to? And you run away.'

'Then you get shot,' Mia said.

'You might get shot anyway.'

'Yeah, but this is different,' his Dad said. 'It's called being a deserter. It's way worse to be shot that way than the other way.'

Ben thought about dessert. Usually in restaurants they did not get one. His Dad had ice cream in the freezer. They could have some later.

'What if you shoot the person who's making you do all the fighting? Like when everyone's shooting, you get them?'

'Then you're a murderer,' Mia said. 'Right, Dad?'

'It's called fragging,' he said. 'It's the worst you can do.'

'But it could stop the fighting for everyone,' Ben said.

'Not for long. I don't like this talk, Ben. Deserting, fragging your CO. These are crimes. You're there to serve. You do your duty.'

'You would be one terrible soldier,' his sister said.

'You would be worse. You'd start crying before it even started,' Ben said.

'Both of you stop. I don't want to talk about it,' their Dad said. 'Let's just order.'

They were not supposed to talk about it. But his Dad had brought it up and Ben had more questions. Had he shot anyone when he was there? Had he been scared? Was he going back? Had he ever wanted to desert or frag or just say stop this, let's just talk about what's wrong? At home when he and his sister fought, that's what his mother said. We don't fight in this house. We talk about what's wrong. We don't do that either, Ben thought.

'When you're older we can talk about it, maybe,' his Dad said, waving the waiter over. 'Right now, stop thinking about it. There's nothing you can do. Don't worry about things you can't fix. Remember that. Just be grateful for what you've got.'

His Dad was confusing him. First he said worry about big things, then he said stop worrying about them. First he was loud, then he went away, and then when he came back he was sometimes quiet and sometimes loud and couldn't stay at home. Now he was saying be grateful for what you've got. Which was what? One annoying twice-as-old sister who interrupted everything just so their Dad would agree with her. A mother who would not let them go beyond the front yard because some stupid kid nearly got hit by a car. And now they got their Dad back, but only at the weekend. They got to go out to restaurants, which was supposed to be a good way to get reacquainted, he said, but was mainly boring. They were in a Chinese restaurant in a not great part of the city. It was a treat. It wasn't anyone's birthday or special occasion. We can treat ourselves for no reason, his Dad had said, when Ben asked why they were going. It's just a good thing to do. Don't worry about it. I don't get a lot of time with you, he told them. So let's make it count.

The spring rolls were too hot and they were the wrong shape. Too big and messy to hold. The grease coated Ben's mouth and the feeling was still there when he was eating the chicken fried rice which was also just kind of slimy.

He was thinking about wet and greasy food and desserts and war when Mia started banging her fist on the table. Her mouth was open like she was trying to breathe in a lot of air but it wasn't working. She reached for a glass but she missed and knocked it over. She put her hands to her throat and her eyes were wide like she was searching for something. She wasn't making any noise. Like she was underwater and couldn't come up for air.

Ben wanted to stand up and go to her and help but his legs wouldn't let him. It was like they were saying sorry, we're not getting involved. We're just jelly sticks and you're stuck to the chair. He watched her eyes go wider.

His Dad jumped up from his chair and got behind her. He put his hands around her stomach and started squeezing her in jolts, one, two, three, each with a silent second in between while Ben watched, pinned into his chair. On four, something came flying out of her mouth and landed on the table. It was grey and wet. About the size of a small eraser.

'You're OK,' his Dad said, standing over her. 'Drink some water. Jesus. Are you OK?'

She was still heaving up and down as she drank the water. His Dad was heaving too, in time with her. Ben was able to stand up now, finally his legs were listening to him again. He went over to her but she pushed him away.

'Stop crowding me,' she said.

He sat back down. Some people had come over to their table to look at what was happening, also crowding her. Ben thought she might say go to hell or get out of my face but she didn't have the energy maybe.

'Are you alright?' the waiter asked. 'What happened?'

'No, she's not alright,' his Dad said. 'She was choking. On one of your bones,' he said, pointing to the grey stub on the table. It was mixed in with the rest of her dinner like it was completely innocent. The waiter said he would get the manager.

'Drink some more water,' their Dad said.

'Should we go to the hospital?' Ben asked.

'Quit bugging me. I'm fine,' Mia said. She was always saying things like this to him. Stop worrying about things. Everything is fine. This is normal. She said all this to him, usually in the bunk beds in the room they shared at their Dad's apartment. She doesn't really know how anything is, Ben thought. She's fifteen and thinks she knows everything. She is twice as old as me but it won't always work like that. That's just the way it is right now. The manager came over.

'The choke lady, yes? I heard what happened. I'm so sorry, are you alright?'

'Yes,' she said.

'She wasn't a minute ago,' his Dad said to the manager.

'Do you want a doctor, we can—'

'No, we don't need that. We're over it now. Right?'

'Right,' Mia said.

'I want to apologise,' the manager said.

'I thought these were boneless wings,' his Dad said. 'We ordered boneless.'

'They are supposed to be,' the manager said, looking at the plate with the bone in the middle. 'An actual wing must have gotten in. I don't know what to say.'

'I'm not happy about this,' his Dad said. 'Imagine if – I mean? Takes a split second.'

'I understand,' the manager said. 'I would not be happy either.'

Ben watched as the two men agreed about not being happy. When his Dad was not happy it did not mean he was sad. It meant something really different. If something was started that made him unhappy his Dad would finish it absolutely, no problem. If someone was treating him with disrespect then he would go deal with it and come back later. It was like he had come back a new harder person because of the metal in him. Or maybe he had always been like this, and Ben had as usual not been paying attention, or couldn't really remember what he was like before he went. He wanted to say to the manager, you better do something about the unhappy feeling. Imagine if, he thought. If their Dad had been in the bathroom or outside making a call. A few seconds ago everything was fine and then her eyes were wide and there was no noise coming out of her and I was like a deserter, I didn't do anything to help.

'What can I do,' the manager asked, 'to make this right?'

'I don't know,' his Dad replied. To Ben it sounded like I'm not the one who should have to think of things to do. My daughter was choking. You figure it out.

Ben looked at his sister. Her face was the normal colour again. It had gone red when it happened. Not cartoon red. Like when someone eats a chilli or something and their face goes tomato and a whistle appears over their head and steam comes out of their ears and their eyes pop out. Then they are fine the next second. They are not real, his mother told him when he was smaller. He knew that, he wasn't stupid.

'There's no charge. For your meal.'

'That's not necessary,' his Dad said.

'I insist.'

'If you insist, then I will not insult you by refusing.'

'And if you guys need a taxi. If you want to take her to – just to make sure,' the man said.

'We appreciate the gesture,' his Dad said. 'But we drove.'

The waiter came over to clear the table. His Dad said they would take the leftovers home for later. Mia opened a tissue and put the bone inside it, and put it in her bag.

'Why would you want to keep it?' Ben asked her.

'Why don't you just leave me alone?' she said.

'It's OK, Ben,' his Dad said. 'She's just upset. It's been a lot.'

'I think we should throw it out,' Ben said to his Dad, when he was putting the food in the fridge back in his apartment. 'What if there are more bones?'

And what if one of us decides to have a late snack, on our own in the kitchen, and another bone goes down the wrong way, he was wondering. What if nobody is there to jolt the other and get it out? Imagine if.

'Don't be dumb. What are the chances of it happening again,' Mia said. 'Two bones in boneless wings?'

'We can check it over before we eat it,' his Dad said. 'And she's right. Odds are—'

'Million to one?' Mia said to their Dad.

'You'd have to be really unlucky,' her Dad confirmed.

'I'm not hungry anyway,' Ben said. He'd had some of the ice cream from his Dad's freezer. It had crystals on the top which he scraped off. The ice cream let him know again, in case he forgot, that his tooth was still there and it was not going away. He was going to say something but with everything, with his sister, it was just not the day for him to have a problem.

★

They were in the bunk beds in his Dad's place. He was on the bottom. There was zero possibility of him sleeping on the top. *Zero possibility*, Mia said when they first saw the bunks a few months ago on their first weekend there, in the new arrangement. I pull rank, she said. I'm twice as old as you. Maybe on my birthday we can swap, he had said to her. Yeah, I'm not falling for that, she said. We swap and then you think that's that. No, just for the night, he said. Then we can go back. I'll think about it, she said. They didn't swap on his birthday because it was a Tuesday and they were only there on weekends and anyway she hadn't agreed, she'd only said she'd think about it.

'Were you scared?' he asked, from the bottom to the top. 'When it was happening.'

'I didn't have a chance to be,' she said.

'What did it feel like?'

'I couldn't breathe. I don't know. Like things were starting to go black.'

'Like falling asleep?'

'Falling asleep really fast and bad.'

'Imagine if Dad had not been there.'

'Yeah. I was lucky.'

'I was just looking at you and I couldn't move.'

'Doesn't matter. Dad knew what to do.'

'Maybe he learned it in the war.'

'Maybe. Don't tell Mom about it.'

'Why not?'

'Just. She will have a freak-out.'

'But don't you want her to—'

'She will have a freak-out. I'm saying. And she might not let us stay here on the weekends or something. So. Keep it to yourself.'

'What if my tooth comes out in the night and I choke on it,' Ben said to her.

'That doesn't happen,' she said.

Their Dad dropped them back to their mother's the next day. He didn't want to come in.

'I'll just wave from the car,' he said. 'I need to keep moving. Jobs to do.'

'Remember, my throat, my business,' Mia said, when they were ringing the doorbell.

Ben did as he was told. There was no point bringing on another freak-out. There had been many freak-outs, like when Dad came back and was shouting in the night, and could not stand it, when their mother told them he can't be here right now, when they agreed they needed time, when he and his sister were told there was a new arrangement, and that's how it was going to be. It was not a forever thing. We'll be OK, Mia said to him. Just deal with it. It's not forever. Like she knew. The bunk situation was not going to change, zero possibility, so why would anything else.

His tooth hurt him all week. Don't be soft about it, he thought. People have worse problems. It could be a war. Just push it out. But it wouldn't come loose.

'What is the softest thing you can eat?' he asked his Dad the next weekend. They were in a different restaurant. His Dad didn't want to go back to the Chinese place.

'Why do you want to know the softest thing?' his Dad asked.

'My tooth is still hurting.'

'Let me look.'

He opened his mouth and his Dad grabbed his jaw and peered in.

'Another one is pushing through. It'll probably just fall out itself. Or I can yank it for you.'

'No.'

'Be over in a second.'

'I don't want that.'

'Well, then you've got to work around it.'

'So what should I get?'

'Soup maybe.'

'It'll be too hot.'

'Or, I don't know. I guess you think ice cream.'

'I don't want ice cream for dinner.'

'Well that's good, because you can't. Anyway we have some at home.'

'What did you eat? When you were in the war.'

'Whatever they gave us. You don't think about food, Ben. Time like that,' his Dad said.

'Stop that noise,' Mia said to him that night in the bunks. She banged on the ladder and woke him. 'Stop it.'

'Stop what?'

'You're grinding your teeth. Stop doing it.'

'I wasn't.'

'You were doing it in your sleep.'

'I didn't know.'

'Well, you were. That's what's making them sore.'

Ben tried to keep still. Don't talk about things. Don't worry so much.

'Why did it happen again? You said it was a million to one.'

'Just, really bad luck.'

This time he had been ready. When she started to pound the table and shake in the restaurant earlier, he told his legs to shut up. He jumped up and went over to her and went behind her like he'd seen his Dad do.

'Leave it,' his Dad said.

He watched his Dad jolt her again, exactly the same as before. One two three and then on four it flew out. This time it was a bit off a plastic fork, like a thin white fang. His Dad had been outraged. I'm outraged, he said to the woman. How could you let this happen? She had been very sorry about it, like the man in the Chinese restaurant. She had not charged them, and his Dad said that he appreciated the gesture, again, and the money was not necessary but thank you and no we won't need to take this further. His sister's face had looked different this time. The first time her eyes were more wild, as if she was saying I don't know what is happening, I don't know anything, it's like I have just been born. This time her eyes had looked more normal, she was looking at their Dad while it was happening.

'Maybe you have something wrong with you,' Ben said up to her bunk.

'There's nothing wrong with me.'

'You could have a bad throat. Or allergies or something.'

'Guess it's possible,' she said. 'There are a lot of allergies going around.'

'Are there?'

'Yeah. They're in the air. They're airborne. That's why you should never sleep with your mouth open. And why you should stop grinding your teeth.'

'Why did Dad say you did good?'

'When did he say that?'

'In the car. After the restaurant.'

'I don't know. Like, I did good not to panic, maybe.'

'Did you keep the plastic?'

'Huh?'

'You kept the bone, last time. Did you keep the plastic?'

'What's interesting about a piece of a stupid fork?'

He lay looking up at the board above him in the bunk. It could collapse. It was not well put together. His Dad and a guy had done it. They were mainly drinking when they were doing it and if he moved too much it creaked loudly. The top could come down and crush him. He'd have to get jolted back to life maybe. He tried not to move too much. If you're in a war any sudden movement can give you away, his Dad said. Stay quiet be still don't ask so many questions. He closed his mouth.

'It's time for a celebration,' their Dad said, the next weekend.

'What are we celebrating?' Ben asked him.

'We don't need a reason,' his Dad replied. 'But if you want one, I had a good week at work.'

'I thought you didn't work,' Ben said.

'Oh, is that what your mother is saying?'

'No, she's not saying anything, Dad,' Mia said.

'Just because it's not regular hours and I don't put on a suit and a tie. When I work, believe me, I am working.'

'We believe you,' Mia said quickly.

'Jobs are plentiful if you apply yourself,' he said. 'Problem is, a lot of people think they have what it takes. Then the rubber meets the road and turns out, they don't. Find the right guy, who actually shows up and does what he says. I'm that guy. We're those guys. So, cheers to us.'

He handed Mia a can. 'Don't tell your mother,' he said.

'You're not supposed to drink beer,' Ben said to Mia.

'Oh, hello,' she said to him. 'Open up it's the boring police.'

'She's nearly sixteen. If this was France,' his Dad said.

'This is not France,' Ben said.

'If you're in the army they say if you're old enough to die for your country, you're old enough to have a drink. Right, Dad?' Mia said.

'You're not old enough for either,' Ben said to her.

'Well, obviously. We're just saying different people have different ideas,' his Dad replied.

'It's not beer anyway,' she said. 'It's cider. So that's nothing.'

'Just some people, having a drink at the end of the day. Most natural thing in the world,' his Dad said, pouring himself some brown liquid and putting in ice cubes from a red bucket. 'I got you a Coke,' he said, taking a bottle out of the fridge for Ben.

'I don't like the taste.'

'That's crazy. Everyone likes the taste. What are you, Russian?'

He drank some of it, to be part of the celebration in not France or Russia or the army and not to be the boring police. It was too cold and sweet and he put his hand on his jaw to feel the throb.

'Still with this tooth?' his Dad said.

'Yeah.'

'If it's not gone by next weekend I'll bring you to my guy.'

Which guy, Ben wondered. Sometimes his Dad took them to a guy who was just a talker. They would have to sit in a bar while he talked to him. His sister was interested in what they were saying and would go up and try to listen in. Ben just wanted to go. I'm at work here Ben, his Dad would say. This is my office. It was just some dark bar. Sometimes there were other kids there, drinking Cokes and acting like this was all normal. He didn't want to go and see one of those guys.

'My guy is great,' his Dad said.

'Is he a dentist?'

'The best. Old school.'

'It might be gone by then,' Ben said.

Mia and their Dad drank.

'When you were a baby, you had a lot of teething trouble,' his Dad said to Ben, topping up his drink. 'I mean, a lot. You used to yell the walls off.'

'Did I?' Ben thought about yelling at a wall so hard that it blew off. If he did that here, they would see right into the next apartment. The old lady next door would look in at them, watching TV or eating her dinner. She might say, come on in, now that there's no wall, if you want.

'Oh yeah. You were crazy.'

'Did I do that, Dad?' Mia asked.

'I don't remember. I think you kind of put up with it more.' His Dad drank the brown liquid. 'This was the only thing that would stop you crying,' he said to Ben, holding up the glass.

'Whiskey?' his sister said.

'Yep.'

'You gave me whiskey?' Ben said.

'Sure did. We put it on a little white rag.'

'Why?'

'Numbs the gums. And then some. Boy did you sleep after that.'

'Great. So I was a drunk baby.'

'Nah. Just a restful one.'

'So, not so perfect now. Drinking whiskey when you were a baby,' Mia said to Ben. 'Explains a lot.'

Ben looked at the two of them. He looked at the bottle on the counter.

'What kind?'

'Huh?'

'What kind of whiskey did you give me.'

'What a weird question. The cheap kind. What, we're going to put some twelve-year-old Scotch in a baby?'

'You're not supposed to do that,' Ben said.

'Oh, what. Everyone did it. Back then. Do that kind of thing now and the world is ... people are way too in your business.'

Ben left them in the kitchen. He sat on his bunk and looked on his iPad. *Is whiskey for babies OK. What happens if you choke. Can you choke on a tooth. Why do people split up. How to pull a tooth. How to know someone if you can't see their face.* One time on the news there was a video of a robbery in a restaurant. The man's face had a mask but he had a way of moving his arms, flexing them. Stay still. Keep your mouth closed. Don't ask questions.

Mia came into their room. 'We're going out to eat,' she said to Ben.

'Now? Why?'

'What a dumb question. Because we're hungry.'

'We've got food here.'

'Do you have to get in the way of everything?'

'I don't want to go out.'

'Well, you can't stay here on your own, Whiskey Baby.'

They were in a diner kind of place. The signs said *Eat and Get Out. Free Smells. Lousy Tippers Go To Hell.* Ben knew they were supposed to be jokes but it all sounded kind of mean. On the wall were photos of customers. *Can you beat the Gutbuster,* the sign over them said. *Free if you finish it.* The people in the photos all had massive cartoon-sized burgers in front of them. They were putting on faces like, oh my God how am I going to manage all of this, it's just too much. And someone from the restaurant was in each photo, pointing at the Gutbuster and laughing, like they were saying well you asked for it, it's your problem if you can't get through it. Each picture had a red sticker on it. *Busted,* the stickers said. They couldn't handle it, his Dad said. Some people just don't know their limits.

'I don't like this place,' Ben said.

'You can get waffles, if you want. How about that. Soft on your teeth.'

'Or put some whiskey on a little rag for him,' Mia said.

He ordered the waffles, even though he wasn't hungry. They all ate.

'All good,' his Dad said. He whispered something to Mia and she nodded.

They are really good friends, Ben thought. Always some kind of little conversation going on. And I'm not in on it. It is rude to leave people out of things. It is not good to be the one who doesn't know what is being talked about. He got up to go to the bathroom.

'Don't go now,' his Dad said. 'Wait.'

'But I need to.'

'Don't stall.'

'You took your time,' his Dad said when he got back to their booth.

'Sorry.'

'Do you want to order anything else?'

'No. Let's just go.'

'Are you ready to go, Mia?' his Dad said. Ben looked at his sister. She had a tissue in her hand, on her lap.

'Don't do it,' Ben said to her.

She did it anyway and her eyes got buggy again and she grabbed her throat. It looked all wrong. Not like the videos he had watched. 'My God,' their Dad shouted, 'She's having a reaction. She's going into shock.' He was taking something out of his pocket and sticking it in her leg. Ben didn't stand up this time. Their waitress came over. She didn't help them or start yelling. She just looked at them.

'Let me see that,' she said to Ben's father, in a very calm way. 'Let me see your EpiPen.'

'My daughter is – are you – she's having a – ?'

She grabbed it out of his hand.

'This is eyeliner,' she said, looking at it. 'You were going to give her a shot of smoky eyes?'

Mia was looking at her father. She stopped shaking and took her hands down from her throat. Her eyes were not buggy but they were still saying, what is going on. Her father looked up at the waitress.

'I must have, in my panic—'

'You must have, what.'

'In my panic. Reached for the wrong thing.' He was looking in his pockets but not taking anything out.

'In your panic.'

'She's OK now. False alarm.'

Mia was looking at the waitress.

'I'm fine, now,' Mia said. 'I thought, there were peanuts. I'm allergic.'

'No peanuts in the ribs,' the lady said. 'Unless you put them in yourself.'

The waitress and Ben's Dad looked at each other. They both looked like they were not happy, Ben thought.

'Wait just – we're not those people,' his Dad said.

The waitress took the tissue from Mia's hand and opened it up, and looked at her, then at Ben's Dad.

'So. What to do with you,' she said.

'I don't like your tone,' his Dad said.

'I could call the police. You won't like their tone either.'

'We will pay,' his Dad said. 'Let's – we don't want any—'

'Sure. You don't want any. Who does? Tell you what. You kids, come over here with me. While Ray here has a conversation with your father.'

Ray looked like a big steak with small eyes, Ben thought. He sat down in the booth beside their Dad. Ray looked like he could make it through a Gutbuster, and then waffles, and a lot of whiskey, and then fight a war and then do whatever he wanted. He didn't look like someone you said *I don't like your tone* or *don't worry about things* to. The waitress brought Ben and his sister to another table.

'So this isn't your first time,' she said to them.

'I have allergies,' Mia said and started crying.

'My daughter has allergies. I know what it looks like. You, missy, are one bad actress.'

Mia put her hands up to her face and said nothing.

'I've seen a lady fake break her waters. I've been held up with a toy gun. But this,' she said, holding up the eyeliner in one hand, and the tissue in the other. 'This is a first. And I've never seen someone use their kids like that.'

'He isn't using me,' Mia said from between her fingers.

'Are the police coming?' Ben asked.

'Depends on how cooperative your father is.'

Their father was cooperative and left a very large tip for the lady. And he gave some cash to Ray for his troubles.

'Well, we really appreciate it,' the lady said to his Dad. 'Now. Let's get a picture of you guys. For our wall here. Ray will take it. Slide up, I want to get in there.'

Ray took the picture. The lady held up the eyeliner and the tissue with the peanut in it. Ben wondered if there would be a special sticker for it.

'We'll be sure to get that out there,' the lady said to their Dad. 'Now, it's time you were leaving.'

They slid out of the booth. As they were going, the lady put her hand on their Dad's shoulder.

'You ought to be ashamed of yourself. Doing that. To your own children.'

'You don't know,' he said to her. 'You don't know anything.'

★

97

'We picked a bad place,' his Dad said on the way home. 'I didn't like the atmosphere in there. That lady was just rude.'

'Yeah. It wasn't a great place,' Mia said.

'They were just not good people.'

'Maybe we should just eat at home in future,' she said. 'Or for a while, instead. What do you think, Dad?'

'I don't give up on things,' his Dad said to her. 'We'll raise the stakes.'

'I hope you don't choke anymore,' Ben said to his sister, in the bunks that night.

'It's unlikely,' she said.

'I watched videos of people choking.'

'That's not right.'

'And people having allergic reactions. It's really bad. Your tongue swells up and you go red. You can be dead in five minutes.'

'Why would you watch that?'

'So I would know what to do. If it happened to you.'

'I don't have allergies.'

'I wanted to be ready, just in case.'

'I was going to be OK. I was always going to be OK,' she said.

'Do we not have enough money? To pay for it?' Ben asked her.

'It's not about that.'

'I told the lady. That you were going to do it.'

'Yeah. I know.' She is not dumb. She maybe thinks I am, but she's wrong, he thought. I'm not dumb and I'm not going to be left out of things.

'Are you going to tell him?' he asked her.

'No. He thinks I made a mess of it. We won't be doing it again.'

'Why did you do it?'

She didn't answer him. Because he likes her more, Ben thought. He's making her. She wants to do things for him. She wants to be like one of those guys he likes.

'What does raise the stakes mean?' he asked her.

'I'm not sure.'

'You're just not telling me.'

Ben got up and went to the kitchen. He opened the whiskey and dabbed some on a tissue. He wedged it at the back of his mouth to cover his tooth. He felt the burning liquid drip down his throat. He wanted to gag, but he held it down. Maybe he would choke and his Dad would wake up and jolt him. Maybe he would sleep better afterwards. You did the right thing, the lady had said. You see something wrong, you say something. I'll deal with it, she said. You don't have to worry. That's not fragging, that's not deserting. That is doing your duty.

He went into his Dad's room. He was asleep. He was snoring loudly and his mouth was open. I could wake him, Ben thought. Say to him, you are not one of those right guys. You should give up on some things. If you're drunk you don't know what's real. Get drunk and go into the war and shoot some people and come home and keep fighting. That is not what you're supposed to do. Or he could pour more whiskey into him. See if he starts choking. Jolt him and bring him back to life and then he would say I'm OK now Ben. I'm fine. He left the room and went back to his bed.

In the morning, when he reached his tongue back, there was a gap. He couldn't feel it anywhere in his mouth, and it wasn't on the bed. If you swallow a tooth it will just dissolve. You can't choke on it. He had looked it up. He thought about his baby teeth. There were still a good few left. They would all fall out. All the pain and trouble getting them, the rags of whiskey and the yelling at the walls, and they were all going to go anyway. Kind of a waste, he thought. He went out to the kitchen. There was a note on the counter. *Had to go out. Get a taxi home.* There was money beside it.

They walked back up the driveway after the taxi pulled off.

'This didn't happen,' she said. 'None of it. Don't even think about telling her.'

It's her problem if she doesn't want to know what's real, Ben thought.

'I can do what I want,' he said. 'You're not in charge.'

'Next time, you can go in the top bunk,' she said. 'For keeps. I'm not kidding.'

'I don't think we should go there anymore,' he said.

Mia turned to him.

'Look. There are people, OK? They don't like him, he doesn't like them. It's not a big deal. Everyone has people who don't like them. But he's – he's still, you don't know. He just – there are things he has to – you don't understand.'

'You sound like him.'

'I can't, stop doing it,' she said, rubbing her eyes. 'I don't know how.'

Something is trapped, Ben thought. Someone is trapped in there. Save one person in a war. He put his arms around his sister, and jolted her, one, two, three. *Get out. Get out of her. Get out of here.*

START IN JAN

UNEXPECTED ITEM.

What were you expecting? Were you hoping for something else? Weren't we all.

DO YOU WISH TO CONTINUE?

And if I say no, where do we go from here. Do you have a better plan? Don't be a fool, Janet. You're the one with the plan. The checkout doesn't care about it. *DO YOU WANT TO PROCEED WITH THIS TRANSACTION?* it's asking now. I've done something shocking awful to the bagging area and it won't stop banging on about it in that tinny estuary tone.

Who does the checkout voice in Tesco. We looked it up on the couch one night. She was in *EastEnders.* Forget her name. What did they say to her in the audition? *Can you sound a bit more disappointed? Like there have been unexpected items all day and you are just at the arse end of your wits and if one more person does a number on your area you'll extend a mechanical arm and feck them out of the checkout?* Was this her last great role? Did she fall down the ranks and land on Vauxhall Bridge in her own bagging area after buying a naggin of Tesco vodka from herself? I like the sound of her begging in my head.

PLEASE CALL FOR ASSISTANCE.

I don't need assistance. I know what I'm doing. I could just leave it. Abandon the basket and walk away. But I've come this far. I've plans for these carrots. They'll play their part in a brutal regime change starting today. Chopped to bits and thrown into a small plastic hell-dome, first but not last victim in the slasher movie in my head, along with these rosy-cheeked apples, this alien's foetus of ginger, and this stupidly large bag of kale. This thing that nobody in their right mind wants that's only sold in units of enormous. Get over it Jan. Climb this kale mountain, get to the top and finish what you're about to start. Four months nine days.

Hello little girl. Are you the assistance? God help us all. 'You keyed in the wrong quantity,' she's saying to me. 'You should have pressed 2 not 1.'

What does she think, I was trying to steal a carrot? I can pay for my carrots, both of them. I don't live in a ditch. I'm not going to bugs bunny them in a car park. I'm bad at maths but I know that 2 is not 1. I'm a teacher I'll have you know, young lady. Home economics not maths, luckily for my students. *Janet Mullen, you are Bad At Maths. Why did you subtract instead of adding? What planet are you from?* This one Sister. *I'm not sure you are. Visit Planet Janet where everything's subtracted until there's nothing left.*

We can't say things like that now. Now it's all *each of you has unique skills and talents* and *it is about reaching your potential.* It really isn't though. It's about knowing your limits and staying well within them. Back to school tomorrow to pander to them with more sweet nothings per the new curriculum. I reached my limit, last time I was in front of the fifth years, when I started back last September. You know what, I said to them, you all need some straight talking. Some of you, well – there's nothing going on up there. And there's no amount of transition year placements in Paris that will light the burner. So you better learn something useful. You're in the only class that matters, ladies. Home Economics. Get out your books. Page 1. Learning outcomes. You, with your head in the sky, read out the first one. *The student will learn to make positive and healthy lifestyle choices.* Get it, girls? Learn to take care of yourselves. Because there's a good chance nobody else will. Oh they'll say they will and then they'll leave and what will you do then? Answer me missy, what will you do when you're all alone?

Straight back it went to their parents and down to Mr MacDonald's office I was sent like a bad one. *Maybe Janet you've come back too soon. Maybe you need more time to … why don't we aim for January.* I want to work, I told him. I need to. *We'll see you when you're ready. You're one of the good ones Jan.* I know that. I'm not, Mr Mac. But I am getting ready. Four months nine days.

The student makes informed decisions and develops good consumer skills. I saw this little assistant sneak a look in my basket as she keyed in her store override code. I do it too. Look in someone's basket, look into their life. This one behind me, with her gin her Pringles her slab of Galaxy. I know what she has in store tonight. I've done my stint on the couch too but I'm up and moving now. Herself with her Pampers, Aptamil, Calpol. From the one aisle I don't go down. I walked down the other one, and we kept on going, longer than many, until we came to the end. *The student deals with unexpected developments and adapts her plans according to circumstances as they present themselves.* How do I present at the checkout? Another dry Jan juicer, barrel shape, barrel end of her forties. Why bother, she'll be back in the sweeties aisle next week. She's no smoothie queen, she's the Blob.

Yes, I know you call me that, girls. You should hear what we call you in the staffroom. I can't argue with it. I let myself go but I'm on the way back. Get back down to fighting weight. I'm back to school tomorrow, fresh start, turn the page ladies. *The student takes action to safeguard and promote her well-being.* Yes, I wish to continue. Contactless. Touch nothing and nobody. Until I'm ready.

Out of Tesco up Henry Street. They should get the lights down quick-smart after the big hoo-ha. Switch them off at the mains lads. Christmas is over, flick, back to work everyone. That was just a warm red dream, greetings to the season of cold dark and wet. We used to go all out on decorations. I kept coming home with more tat. *Is there such a thing as too much tinsel? Not on Planet Janet*, you said. It was a modest display by any standard this year. Honour you with stars and a few strands of silver. All glad tidings are gone out of me. Planet Janet's gone once more around the sun, drifting further out of orbit. I caught a blobby reflection in a bauble last night as I stripped away the last of the glitter. By midnight all the bits were back in their boxes and up to the attic. That's where I got the lump on the head. A knock on the forehead and a door opened and now I know what I'm at. *Knuckle the fuckle down now Jan.* Blob to Belter in four months nine days. Get into Arnotts. Get a blender. *The student demonstrates that they can use appropriate tools and technology to achieve their goals.*

You used to call it *the most solid shop in Dublin.* Used to be for communion dresses and curtains but they've upped their game, haven't they? That was another one of your sayings. *I've upped my game Jan*, any time you did something that passed for a chore half done. I talk like you now, in my head at least. I listen for you and I talk for you. I take it one day at a time but I'm picking up the pace. This one's not over but quarter to six on a Sunday, well we are in the fag end of the weekend and January is in on us brutally. Back to school tomorrow and a new plan, starting tonight: buy fresh vegetables, crush them, drink and be well. I need my strength for what's ahead. Reset and recover. First from the unexpected item in the forehead area.

Caught me dead centre. Down it came and walloped me, a solid silver frame, one of many useless wedding presents. We should have done a list. We should have registered here at Arnotts. *Ah no*, you said. *Let's not be like that. People can get what they want.* That's not the right approach, I thought, but that que sera in you, maybe I could try it on. *Don't try to control things, Jan. You'll do your head in, and mine. Go with the flow.* That's how we ended up with five silver picture frames. *Let's melt them down,* you said, *we'll have riches.* Let's return them, I said. We'll have actual money. One of them came preloaded with a picture of a happy couple, holding hands on a beach, bare-foot in denim shirts and white trousers, leaning into each other, smiling pearly eternal, a golden-blond boy between them. We kept that one. We left them in the frame and put it on the mantlepiece for a lark. Laura and Lenny you called them. *How are you there now, Laura and Lenny. Aren't you having a grand day on the Strand? Show me and Jan the way to beachful bliss and may the sand stay out of your lily-white pants forever amen.* We called each other Laura and Len, for a while. But like your prayer, it didn't stick. We weren't like them. We never gave a name to the boy.

The student will learn how to prepare balanced meals for themselves and those around them. Take this down ladies, an easy-to-follow recipe: Take two bodies; combine, bind and blend until the texture is warm and yielding; let set gradually for a few years. Do not leave it too late to start. Do not cool completely. Do not allow fat to settle on the surface. Don't fight about stupid things that do not matter, and that's most things. Every day wasn't silver picture-perfect Len. I know that. We fell out of the frame many's the day. *All you can ask is more good days than bad.* What was the final tally?

I put us in the frame beside Laura and Lenny. I wrapped it and gave it to you on our first wedding anniversary. A picture of us on Curracloe Beach. We were going to recreate the famous shot, but you said you couldn't risk being seen in white trousers, not even in Wexford. You held out your phone and took the photo at arm's length. We're at forty-five degrees, my head is cut off at the top. Dutch angle you said it was called. I looked it up and you're right. I'm like a baddie in one of those superhero movies you were obsessed with. There was an order to watch them in, you insisted. *It's not the order they came out in. There's a lot of debate online.* I don't think it matters, I said, but on you'd go about the layers and the connections and the *universe*. We didn't get through them all together but I've kept the faith. There's a new *Justice League* series starting tomorrow and I'll watch that too but God's sake they're all the same. Someone loses something dear to them, discovers their power, builds their strength, rises up, avenges, leaves room for a sequel. *The student brings an idea from concept to realisation.*

I'm sliced off on Curracloe but your face is fully in the frame, late day sun in your eyes. *May we always have bliss like L&L and who knows who else xx*, I wrote on the card. You didn't approve. *Oh my God. Are we them now?* It's just a little joke, I said. *It's too much pressure, Jan.* We ate in silence, until you said: *About the whole – I know you want to. I just. Can we just leave it, a while?* How long did you think we had? We were late enough finding each other. We should have moved when the market was down, but you wanted to stay put. I wanted to start, you wanted to wait, and then we were told. *Nothing can be done,* you said. Leave the things that weren't going to happen to pile up and leer down from the mantlepiece, while we sat on the couch and slid into the wine lake. I put Laura and Lenny up in the attic one day, and you never remarked on their absence. Sorry Blissfuls, you're going into cold storage. Your white trousers will go dust-grey along with us. There's no one else coming into the frame. I caught the edge of it with the decorations box last night, and down we all came into my face. Near knocked me off the ladder. My head on fire with a new pulse. First anger boiling, hit back, attack. And then blame. You did this. You left.

Remember what you said to me on the way out that night? *I have to get out of here.* Because I was *at you.* Cop on, I said. The radiators upstairs weren't working, that's all. There are jobs in any house. It was cold, all you need is to bleed them. I'd have done it myself but no you kept saying *I'll do it I'll do it let me be the man about the house.* I got a key and put it on the table. *Ah, mañana mañana, vino time?* you said. No, *now,* I said. If you can't do it, I will. *Belittling* you was I. *I'm no good at this stuff, Jan. You know that.* I did. But I kept pushing. Your Mama did all the jobs and cooking for you. Do you ever think of lifting a finger? Out you stormed and while you were drowning your rad-related sorrows I was bleeding them. It's simple. It's satisfying. There's a hiss and a gurgle and a dark trickle and pressure is equalised. I put a hand on cold white metal and felt the rising warmth of a job done.

The student demonstrates self-sufficiency in a range of household activities. Take note of this girls, there is nothing charming whatsoever in being useless around the house. Was I too pushy? Was I too much? Was I the kind of person that people just want to get away from. Girls in the classroom counting down the days they can turn their back on me. I'm being an idiot, I thought, as I bled the last rad. This is a tiny nothing. Don't make it otherwise. What's a few chores in exchange for bouts of joy and the promise of not being alone. Is that not a fair deal. Let go of what doesn't matter and what will not be, hold on to what is. I left it in a note on the counter and went to bed. *Let there be warmth and let all our troubles be little ones xx* I wrote. But the deal was undone. You were careless to the last. You didn't come in the door, you went to the middle of the road and stayed there.

It wasn't *murder* they said to my screaming face. It wasn't *premeditated.* He was where he should not have been. *The pedestrian was intoxicated and was in the road thus endangering himself. However, a less negligent driver could have averted it, and she must bear responsibility for her actions. In light of her unblemished record and family responsibilities I am handing down* she could have avoided you. And you could have stayed on the path like a normal person. Two of you on a collision course since the start of time like one of your movies. *A conviction of involuntary manslaughter.* She gets one year, you're erased from the universe. Two minus one equals infinity and war. I put a hand on a cold metal frame and felt no warmth. Yes that's him, I said. That was us. Manslaughter. Man's laughter. Slow burn, warm glow, inferno then ashes.

Take all the time you want, I was told at school. I only wanted one thin sliver of time, to start a sentence again. But it was gone. There was support, your family, faces coming into focus through the fog. I did the counselling. A man fresh out of college with round glasses and a jutting chin took me through the gear changes of grief. *You are hurting*, he said, *and you want others to feel it. That is natural.* He said it so evenly, as if not to disturb me from my slumber, like he was observing me from a distance. What do you know about anything, I said to him, that little owl on a cartoon half-moon. *You're angry*, he said. *It's part of the cycle. We will work through it at the pace that's right for you*, he said. But time's against us all, our universal nemesis, laying waste to every half-arsed plan. Keep moving, go through, keep going. If I stall today at the blenders, I may never start again.

So now we'll discuss Bargaining, he said, in our third session. *The student understands the relationship between price and value.* There's only one fair exchange remaining. I am ahead of you, I said. I'm in the blue meadows of acceptance. I don't need any more sessions. Thank you so much for your help. I just wanted to get away. Get back to work.

He was right. It's a cycle. It doesn't end, no matter what order you go through, and now I'm back where I belong, in the red zone. It took a knock to crank me up again but my system is restarting, the boiler's lit. My head was opened on the ladder last night and in went the plan, in the voice that used to soothe me, before it went to sleep. *Wake up Jan. You need to start again.* The party for one is over. Some lingering house guests need to go. Sharing bags of Quavers, unshared. There's the door you dayglo demons. Wine in general, Señor Rioja and Madame Chablis in the specific. *Adios amigos.* I'm by no means thrilled to replace you with vile green sludge but I've a job to do. It starts with health and ends in hell. It starts now with *five minutes to closing* in Arnotts and will end on April the eleventh. We are at the business end, ladies. Multiple choice question. From this shelf of blenders, make a decision. *The student takes initiative and develops entrepreneurial skills.* This one looks like it could pulverise anything I throw at it: kale, bones, silver frames. Magimix 4000. Weight of it. Lugging this in and out of the press every day. Wear me down when I need to stay limber.

This one. Blades look medieval. Will do the job. Pressure has to go somewhere. There is another way. It's called trepanning. Remember we watched a documentary. Sounds like a little springing ballet dance but it's drilling a hole in your head to increase the blood flow. In prehistoric France they found skulls, there are accounts of it from the fourteenth century, they said it opened up new realities it took away pain it gave the mind flight. It was like seeing God, the narrator said. Is that your view now Len. Please tell me what you see. Are you telling me to see this through. Or are your eyes closed in the wet dark cold. I won't look away from this job. I could drill through this bump and bone. Hear the hiss gurgle warm trickle feel myself rise. See what I'm made of. If I put a hole in my head would it bleed you out, would you want me to? *Let me out Jan. I have to get out of here.* Would it let the light in and the darkness out. Let the devil in to do his business. I feel in need of some assistance. Could I do it with the Pulsar 850? Feel the Pulse Power, it says. *The store is now closing, please take your purchases.* Take it to the counter. Come on girl, turn around we are up against it here can't you see my head about to burst if you don't –

'Mrs Mullen?'

Sarah Conlon. Fifth year. She had a bump, before I went off. Not now. What did you choose, Sarah. You had a choice at least, and if another life was going to wreck yours, well, I'm in no place to judge. *The student understands the consequences of their actions on themselves and those around them.* She'll have another chance. Time's not on her back just yet. I'd rather she didn't know my business, but it's closing time and I've no choice.

'I didn't know you worked here, Sarah.'

'Just over the Christmas.'

'Good for you. Working hard.'

'Back in school tomorrow.'

'Me too.'

Don't look so surprised, Sarah. Did you think I'd sink into my couch and never come back? I was waiting for the look of the fifth years when I walked in. That's right, girls. The Blob is back. Now she'll spoil the surprise.

'Will we have you for Home Ec again? Mrs Chambers isn't really, you know—'

'I'm sure she's doing a fine job. Bit of respect, Sarah.'

'Sorry. But you're better.'

'Well, I don't know about that.'

I am better. I'm getting better. Wait till you all see me at my personal best.

'I hope you are feeling, better, Miss. I'm really, I wanted to go to the funeral but my parents said, because of, it was—'

'That's OK, Sarah. I understand. Now if you can just ring me up.'

Swipe slash start crush, come on Sarah, we've no time for sorry now.

'Miss I'm really sorry but the till is locked.'

'What does that mean.'

'It won't let me put it through after six. The system's shut down.'

'But it's only just gone six.'

'But yeah. It's. It won't go through.'

This is what happens when I let time slice away. How hours months years bleed out. What am I thinking. *Janet Mullen what planet are you on.* Get back on that couch. You're not up to the job, you can't even buy a blender. You're no belter you're The Blob *do you have any juice in you at all* I do Sister I do.

'I'll give you cash. You can put it beside the till. Here I'll write a note, say your teacher came in, they'll understand.'

'We're — not allowed to do that.'

Allowed. Have I taught you nothing, child? *Take initiative.*

'I could set it aside for you and tomorrow you could—'

'Sarah. Maybe you can just. Get it out of here for me.'

'What, like—'

'I need this. I really need it now. I can't let it go another day. I'll meet you outside. I'll leave the cash here.'

'I can't. If they caught me, I'd be—'

In she'll go tomorrow and tell them. They'll all have a good old laugh. You won't believe it she asked me to steal a *blender* for her should I tell Mr Mac I think she's gone mad she was always fucking mad remember when she told us we were stupid and all that about binding bodies? Come on her husband was after dying. Don't care, you still can't say that. The fucking Blob with a blender what's she going to do? Make Snickers smoothies? Sarah will ruin it. I can't have that.

'I was only having you on, Sarah.'

'Oh, right.'

'I was testing you. I knew you wouldn't. You're one of the good ones.'

'I thought you were angry with me, Mrs Mullen.'

'There's nothing wrong with being angry.'

'No, I know.'

'Are you angry, Sarah?'

'No, not real—'

'You should be.'

'I'm not sure what . . .'

'You should be. Whoever did it to you.'

'It wasn't, like that.' Look at her rosy face boiling. Come on. Lash out. 'He was going to –'

'Going to what. *Stand by you?* Cop on, will you? Hope he gets what is coming to him.'

Go on girl. Yeah your teacher said that to you. What are you going to do? I'll hold him down for you. It'll be good practice. It'll be your practical. I'll give you an A-star if you fucking crush his nuts.

'I – Miss, are you . . . OK?'

'Yes, good idea Sarah, set this thing aside. That's a good girl. I'll be back in tomorrow. I'll see you in the morning now. Bright and early. New year, new start.'

'Yes, Miss.'

Yes, Miss. You fucked up, Miss. Go home, Miss. Go to the bus stop and give up. You had one job. You couldn't even get started. Any other plans? Swing back into Tesco, invite all your old friends over and all sink back down. Stick on a movie. Spill out on the floor bleed out under the blue light be found by neighbours *we didn't know until we got the smell we thought it was a burst pipe.*

Is that what they all think is going to happen. The Blob's finally burst? Well I'll show you, Sarah. I'll show for you, Len. And I'll show her. Get on the bus. Another day lost but I will be back tomorrow. I've no time to waste. Four months nine days: she's out. I will be at my fighting weight. I will be waiting. The pressure has to go somewhere, you can't keep it in the system. You have to open the valve or it will explode. This vessel in my head is pulsing and what's trapped inside will bleed out of me and onto her. I will show her what *premeditated* looks like when it's at home. A Victim Impact Statement will be delivered to her door and it will be in more than words this time.

That is just the start. Don't expect results day one, girls. Be patient. I could drive over her. But we want this to linger. Get a job at her local café. I know where she lives. Dye my hair, wear a disguise. Play a slow game. Leave it a few months, let her think she's in the clear. Wait until she thinks the knock on the door is never coming, then make her a special blend. Watch her drink it, and as she realises, and clutches her throat, stand over her as the light goes out. *It's me. Look at me. Let me be the last thing you see.* I looked at someone in a cold silver frame and I promised. I will drive a hard bargain for you.

I could take her. Bring her down in here with me. Keep her chained to a radiator. I could force her to look at our photos. Make her take in what she took. Crush metal in the blender and make her swallow the shards. I could wear a mask. What do you think Len? *You're being ridiculous, Jan.* You're right. What would be the point of hiding. She knows who I am, she heard me scream *murderer*, she looked at me and turned away. We'll meet again. There are more phases in the cycle than that multicoloured picture suggested. There are darker shades. Think you served your time? Think you're clean in the eyes of society? They're not looking. When it comes, it'll be just us. My sentence is never ending and she is going to take her share of it.

Start. Start now in the garage. What can a blender do that I can't? I don't need a blade I'll take my carrots and ginger and hulk smash them with a hammer I'll fling them against the garage wall and beat them to a pulp I'll hold an apple to my head and drill a hole in it and feel it approaching bone and I will take flight I'll feel the blood flow I'll see her face in the mess on the floor and I'll lay red waste to her in my head and in my hands and in four months nine days *Len this is for you, do you see?* I do wish to continue you would do it for me. You'd want me to, you'd want me to want this, wouldn't you?

So yes I will come back tomorrow Sarah I'll call in sick and wellness and wrath will rise in me and flow out unstoppable there is a war coming and I will go over the top look into my head if you don't believe see into me and see what I see come in here with me and as we smash through apples bones and brains say with me

Say with me

Scream it on the garage floor with me

Say it with me Len. Say what you used to say. *You are the Justice League Jan. No one can stop you when something gets in your head.*

Say it.

Jan.

I need to hear it in your voice. I need to hear you want me to.

Jan. Listen.

Don't you dare. You started me and ended us. I'm the one who has to go on alone.

It's not going to work.

She could be out already they could have let her out early they could have moved her, they don't have to tell me. I should have been watching. But I'm known to them and I'll never, how could I get near her, there's no chance, I have no chance. But if I don't try then what? What, Len?

Go with the flow. Let the earth turn and hold on for dear life. Stop turning against it.

Don't turn away. Come back. Don't leave me like this.

I have to get out of here. And so do you.

I've nowhere left to go.

Go to sleep Jan. And then wake up.

You need to start again.

PLEASE SAY WHY YOU'RE CALLING

SHE SAW HIM ON THE first day of her assignment. She was walking along the canal bank to the office. He was just ahead of her. She blended into the stream of people on their way to work. Nobody would look at her and think, you are not from here, you don't know where you're going. She knew exactly. She had walked and timed the route over the weekend. Twenty-two minutes from the hotel to the call centre building. She allowed for thirty, to build in margin for error.

She walked in his wake. His arm extended over the statue on the bench as he passed it. It was not a lingering touch. A cup of the shoulder, not breaking pace. As you might do to a friend sat peacefully, so as to acknowledge their solitude and wish them well without disturbing them. Touch a statue for no reason though. Why do that? There's no efficiency to be gained. It is a wasted action. Just today, or every day? Just in the morning, or on the way home too? These were distracting thoughts and not part of the process. In the evening the statue would be warm to the touch, iron limbs baked by the sun, which the man at the hotel reception said might be the best we get all summer, even though it was only April. Enjoy it while it lasts, he said to her. Because it won't.

It sounds like you are asking about your balance, is that right?
I'm sorry, I didn't get that. Please say, in a few words, what
you are calling about.

The target was 24 per cent reduction in Average Call
Handling Time. Go to Dublin, deliver efficiency gains
through the implementation of the Interactive Voice
Response system, move on to the next assignment. She
did not know much about the place. She remembered
the footage of people during Italia '90 four years ago,
jumping in fountains and standing on top of cars, even
though they hadn't won. She had watched the final with
a few friends in her apartment in Bremen. She hadn't
celebrated excessively when her country won. They
were expected to, and a reunified team should do well
again this summer. Maybe Irish people didn't expect
much, so any kind of result was a cause for celebration.
They had won the Eurovision, twice in a row, but
nobody in Germany particularly cared about that.

Six weeks in Dublin on an IVR project: Not exciting.
Not difficult. Not new. But it would be her first solo project.

'You ever been there?' her manager asked her.

'No,' she said.

'Fun city,' her manager said. 'Or, there's a supply chain
analysis in Gdansk.'

'I'll take Dublin,' she said.

'Fun,' her manager said. 'Do it the same as Munich.
Stick to the process.'

There is no issue, she had been told in her orientation,
that cannot be addressed by the process. Agree what
problem we are trying to solve. Identify and align stakeholders. Formulate mutually exclusive and collectively

exhaustive options. Quantify the cost-benefit of each option and choose the optimal. Establish a sense of urgency. Measure outputs. Communicate results. Sustain change. It did not matter if it was reducing handling time in call centres in Dublin or optimising public services in Bavaria. Trust the process. Do not deviate.

'I don't get it. How will you reduce call time that much?' She had expected this question, in the first meeting, when she was setting out the process.

'Through the IVR,' she explained, moving on to the next slide in her presentation. 'It will understand people's queries. If someone needs to know their balance, or when their next payment will come out, it will tell them.' She played the video they'd made in Munich, demonstrating it in action.

'How will it know what they're saying?' someone asked.

'We will train it with samples. It's been very effective in Germany.'

'In Germany. I see.'

'So people won't get through to an agent?' another of them asked.

'Not unless the IVR can't answer their question. In which case their call will go into the Unresolveds Queue.'

'Unresolveds?'

She pointed to a box marked UQ on her chart. UQ was where calls would be sent to die. Anything that did not have a standard answer. There were a lot of those. She'd read the call logs over the weekend in preparation. *Am I going to get cancer from your masts and how can you prove I'm not? You've erected a pole outside my house and I've been parking there for fifteen years and there is such a thing as precedent and rights. Someone keeps turning off my heat at night and*

I live on my own, explain that? Callers stuck in UQ would give up eventually, and call back and try the IVR again. They would learn how to work within its parameters. It is not a question of the IVR expanding to understand more of people's queries, she explained in the conference room in Dublin, as she had in Munich. It is about people learning how to ask the right questions. There are only so many queries in scope. They are mutually exclusive and collectively exhaustive. As long as your question matches our database, we will be able to help you, without involving another person. If it's something else, there will be a very long wait and possibly no answer.

The union rep shuffled in his seat. A man with a scrunched-up red face.

'So, Maria. How much time are you expecting this will save?'

'Scaled up, over two years, we're targeting 18,000 hours. That's what we achieved. In Germany.'

'Or to put it another way. About eight of our members,' he said.

'Headcount reduction is not the objective, Bill,' the centre manager said. 'This will free up time for people to handle more complex queries.'

'Will it, yeah. And what will happen when the robot figures out how to answer those too? Will this fake voice thing tell them where to find another job?'

'The system is called Interactive Voice Response,' Maria clarified.

'I don't care what it's called. It's not going to happen,' Bill said.

They said this in Munich too, she thought. And Stockholm. Protect the workers from automation. Don't let technology take our jobs. They probably said it in the cotton fields in the 1920s. This is the process. The union's concerns would be dealt with. Delay any headcount reductions, initially. It was not her concern what they did with excess capacity in the long run. By the time that maths was done, and outplacement plans were being implemented, she would be a dozen assignments down the road and would never think about where those eight, more likely fifteen, people might go next. It's not your job to make friends, she was told in orientation. People will be against you. That's part of the process.

For fourteen straight days he had touched the statue. She continued to allow thirty minutes for her walk to the office, even though there was no chance of an error. They aligned each morning without fail. Wherever he started his day from, whatever route channelled him onto the path along the canal, it put him two minutes ahead of her each morning. She kept a steady pace, walking through the moment that he had just left. Moments are stationary and people approach then move through them. Sometimes together, sometimes in single file, she thought. She had started to follow his process. Touch the statue on the shoulder. Put my hand where his has just been. It is an experiment, she told herself. That's a reason to do it. Perhaps I will cause a chain reaction. Others behind me will do it too. The Irish were a superstitious people. Believed in fairies and touching wood for luck. Touching a statue could become one of those traditions. Traditions take root in coincidence. Do not conflate causation and correlation, she had been trained. It starts with someone winning money or cheating death and deciding it was the rabbit's foot in their pocket or the tap of a statue on the shoulder. If you press 0 # 0 0 4 1 in the IVR you are automatically routed to an agent. It was the kind of thing Irish people would all tell each other. *Feck the process lads, there's a shortcut.* Any way they could beat the system, they would.

Interesting Development: World Wide Web, the email subject said. *It provides a new way to access information. This could become extremely useful. All colleagues are encouraged to try 'Surfing The Net'. Please limit your time however, as each minute costs.*

She followed the instructions in her hotel room and waited for the page to load. *Where do you want to go today?* it said at the top, as an image of a globe slowly emerged, one horizontal segment at a time. She clicked on one of the underlined blue phrases: <u>Useful information</u>. It took almost three minutes to load another image, of a large *I*, with more underlined blue phrases. She was conscious of the costs, every minute adding up, and unplugged the phone cable.

Where do you want to go today? It was a Friday night in a supposedly fun city and she was not expected to be working all the time. Go for a walk and see what happens, her father would have said. *Spazieren gehen.* There were bars everywhere. She looked in the windows of several. Go in and order a beer. Have some of the *craic* that the people in the office had spoken about. *Spaß machen.* Meet someone. Have an interesting conversation. Fall in with some group and end up at a party. *Oh you're from Germany? And you're here on your own? Come with us and have some fun.* Or end up sitting in at the bar on your own. More likely. Odds of meeting a particular person and asking him some questions were extremely low. Or reject all of these options and go back to the hotel. Have a drink in your room. If that's what you want to do, if that seems like fun. Then get back to work. Collectively exhaustive, mutually exclusive.

'Now that one. Lay my life on it. That's Cork.'

'No. Sounds more Limerick?'

'You're miles off John. If I was to put a pin in it, I'd chance Fermoy. Am I right, Maria? Put us out of our misery.'

These two, assigned to her to assist with voice sampling, were turning this into a guessing game. John and Frank. Team leaders. They'd survive. For now.

'I don't know where they're from,' she said to them. 'It doesn't matter. The point is to identify patterns so we can train the IVR to recognise and respond.'

'Listen. Maria. We were thinking. About your one. The IVR,' Frank said.

'What about it?'

'She's, well. A bit ... Radio 4,' he said.

'I don't know what that means.'

'She's a bit, English, is what that means,' John said.

'*Very* English. I wouldn't be as strong on those but I'd hazard a guess at Hertfordshire,' Frank added.

'It doesn't seem like it matters? If it is answering your question?' Maria said.

'Ah. It does though. See. Your one from Fermoy—'

'—or more likely Abbeyfeale—'

'She's not going to want to hear some disembodied hockey-stick from the home counties telling her what to do,' Frank said.

'We've had a lot of that,' John added.

'It's the standard voice. For English-speaking markets.'

'Yeah. It isn't here,' Frank said.

'What does it matter if you are getting the correct information? Do you think people prefer waiting for ten minutes to hear an Irish voice or getting their information now from an English one?' she asked them.

'I'd have to think about that,' Frank said, 'for a good ten minutes.'

'What would it take to change it, Maria? Doesn't have to be an Irish voice. We're very, multicultural. Up to a point,' John said.

'That's not in scope.'

'Listen. The two of us could do it,' he continued.

'You'd have the voice for it, John,' Frank said.

'It sounds like you'd be somewhere west of the Shannon, is that right?'

'Grand day isn't it?'

'Great drying weather.'

'People would love that, Maria,' Frank said. 'It'd be a nice touch. If you want to talk about the weather for a while, press 1. Bit of a novelty factor?'

'The point is not to have a conversation with people about weather. The point is to give them the information they need efficiently.'

'Have you been to Fermoy, Maria?' said Frank.

They're mocking me, she thought. They think this is just fun. They do not care, or realise, or both. They kept saying it would all just be grand. You're very young to be so serious, they had said. You are too old to be so stupid, she thought.

'I think the problem here is, you're only hearing the first part of the call, Maria,' John said to her.

'That's all we need. We are looking for query patterns,' she said.

'Tell you what. Would you come and listen to some actual calls?'

'Give you more of a feel for it?' Frank said.

'There really is no point. It's not in—'

'In scope. Yeah. Listen though. Might do you some favours. Let people see you're getting stuck in. Not just staying, you know. Up here. In the hallowed halls of the fourth floor.'

Build rapport. Align stakeholders. It could assist the process, she thought. Get away from these two stupid men who did not respect the process, or her. Maria the Robot. She had heard them in the kitchen. *Jesus lads but she's zero craic.*

Would you both like to be fired, is that right?
Press 2 to get new people.

'We like to really build a connection, with our customers,' Frank said to her, as they walked around the call centre floor. 'You know, that human touch.'

He stopped at a cubicle and tapped an agent on the shoulder. 'Javier, this is Maria. She's here to listen in to some calls. OK if she sits in with you for a while?'

'Course, yeah,' Javier said. He handed her a headset. She put it on and sat behind him in his cubicle.

'Can you hear me?' Javier said.

'Yes, I can hear you.'

'I'm waiting for a customer to come back with their reading. So, we can talk. She won't be able to hear you anyway.'

'OK,' she said, talking to him over his shoulder. She could hear him breathing in her ears.

'Where are you from,' she asked him.

'Portugal. You?'

'Germany.'

'Are you joining our team?'

'No. I'm a consultant. Working on a project.'

'Oh. Special person. I better do a good call.'

'No no. Just do what you normally do.'

'Hello, I'm back,' came the voice through the headset.

'Hello Mrs Mulally. Did you manage to get the reading?'

'I did Javier. 5540669.'

'That's perfect thanks. So I've updated that here. Your next bill will show the reduction. So you shouldn't have any more troubles.'

'Great stuff now thanks.'

'Is there anything else I can help you with?'

'Can you give us another win in the Eurovision on Saturday?'

'Ha, yes. I wish I could. I will be working, but I might be able to see some of it. Three in a row maybe for Ireland?'

'I'm sure you lads will do well too. What's your song called?'

'*Chamar a Musica*. Means call the music. Beautiful song,' Javier said to the caller.

'I'll listen out for it.'

'Thank you, and thanks for calling All Energy today. Bye now.'

'Bye yep bye bye bye.'

'You sound quite Irish, when you are talking,' Maria said through the headset.

'You pick it up. They like talking.'

The action of his voice in her headphones was strange, as if he was transmitting directly into her.

'Have you been here a long time?' she asked him.

'About a year. And you?'

'Just a few weeks. I'm not staying long.'

'Oh. Shame. You like it so far?'

'Yes. Fun city.'

'Yes. Very fun.'

Another call was coming in. Someone from Ballinrobe was having a boiler issue. It could be anything next, she thought. There was no flow or routing. He had to answer all sorts of things. It was so inefficient. The ideal process, she thought, was that nobody ever called. Some day that will be how it works. Look up information and never speak to someone.

What could he be asked next. Why do you touch the statue in the morning, Javier? Forget the process. I personally need to understand the nature of your enquiry. Is it for luck? Do you know that your luck will change? Do you know that this centre will not be here in five years? It makes no sense that it is in the middle of an expensive growing city. In the future Mrs Mulally will give her reading to a machine and it will have nothing to say about the Eurovision. Where will you be then, Javier? Will you find another job in this supposedly fun but actually not welcoming place? Or will you take your redundancy as a sign to move on? Will the process change your life? Will you return to Portugal? Will the statue no longer feel a hand on its shoulder in the morning? Will anyone miss you? Is there someone in this city that is for you, or are they all against you, too? I'm inches from you. Do you want to turn around and see me? Could we walk together? This was all well out of scope.

Frank tapped her on the shoulder, a few calls later.

'Heard enough?' he said.

'Yes, thank you.' She took off the headset.

'I hope it was useful for your project,' Javier said.

She shook his hand, and went into the meeting where her objective was to calmly explain to people that he and many others like him would at some future point no longer be necessary. She and Javier were, according to the process, mutually exclusive.

It was Saturday night and she could have been out having fun. But there were samples to analyse, and results to write up. And fun, well fun here meant drunk, as far as she could tell. She had gone out with Frank and John on their one invitation. They had asked her personal questions. How old was she, was there a boy back in Germany. She had not answered, had ignored their questions about union opposition and had failed to drink sufficiently for their liking. They had not invited her out again. It didn't matter. Do not form personal connections. This could subvert the process. The quicker she worked, she thought, the sooner it would be done. So she was in the office, while everyone else was watching the Eurovision and having fun. She emailed a progress update to her manager. The office phone rang.

'I'm sorry. I meant to call you yesterday,' her manager said. 'It's not going to happen.'

'What's not going to happen?'

'The IVR. Union reps have threatened strike action. They are stronger than in other markets. Management are capitulating. For now,' her manager said.

'I've followed the process,' she said.

'They're just not ready for it,' he said. 'I should have scoped it better. Don't take it personally. It's not a reflection on you.'

'I don't like to leave projects unfinished.' It was a reflection. Her first solo assignment, and she'd been bullied into submission. Would she be put in a back-office. Not let loose again.

'We'll come back to them in a few years. By '96, '97 tops, they'll be ready. There'll be an upturn in their economy and people will want to be in other jobs anyway. This will all go offshore. That will be a good project for us.'

'So, am I done here?' she asked.

'Yes. File a closeout report. Note where there were deviations. Lessons learned. You know.'

'I'll start now.'

'You don't have to work the weekend on it. Monday is fine. Have some fun on the weekend, Maria. Then you can come back here next week for your Y2K training.'

'What's Y2K?'

'New initiative. People are worried their systems are going to fail because they can't handle the year 2000. Hospitals will go dark, planes will fall out of the sky, elevators will drop to the floor. That kind of thing.'

'And will they?'

'We don't expect so. But people want to be reassured. We have a new de-risking process. It's very comprehensive. We can apply it anywhere.'

'It's not for six years.'

'Yes. But we want to start generating healthy anxiety now. It is never too early for people to worry about a problem we can solve.'

'And if it doesn't happen? If planes don't fall out of the sky?'

'Then we prevented it, and everyone will be very happy.'

'By that logic, if I touch a statue and I don't spontaneously combust, the statue prevented it.'

'I'm sorry, Maria. The line is not great. You said something about a statue?'

'It doesn't matter.'

'Close up the project. You can come back early. Y2K process training starts Tuesday.'

'I'll be there.'

'Have you had a good time in Dublin?'

'Yes. Fun city.'

'I told you.'

Nobody else was on the fourth floor. Why would they be, on a Saturday night? She'd leave and there would be no need to say goodbye to anyone, and nobody would care when she wasn't there on Monday. She'd walk along the canal back to the hotel and move towards the year 2000 and its impending lucrative problems. She took the lift to the ground floor. She paused in front of the door to the call centre. I could walk in, she thought. I could look at the late shift, people who would never know how close they came. I could say to them, you do not know your luck. Or say it to one person in particular. I do not have a *boy* at present, in Germany, or anywhere. Not that it was anyone's concern. Situations can change quickly though. One day everything is fine, the next planes are falling out of the sky. *Where do you want to go today.*

There is no reason for me to be in here now, she thought. No reason to walk through the cubicles and tap him on the shoulder.

'Maria, hey. Working late?'

'Yeah. Just finishing some stuff.'

'I think we are the only two people in Ireland working tonight,' Javier said.

He pointed to the TV on the wall.

'They are really quite obsessed with it, aren't they?' she said.

'Yes. It's very silly. But because they win, they like it.'

'Yes. Very silly,' she agreed.

'Everyone watches. I'm not going to get many calls tonight. Nobody else wanted the shift so I said fine. Very easy night. Oh, I shouldn't be telling a special person that, perhaps.'

'I don't care. Have an easy night. Why not,' she said. 'I might listen in anyway. Just in case you get a call. If that's OK?'

She sat behind him and put on the headset. They watched the song contest on the TV. She went over and unmuted it.

'We are not meant to have sound up,' he said to her.

'I don't think it matters,' she said.

'Well, if the consultant says.'

'I do. Who is next?'

'Portugal.'

'Good luck,' she said to him.

The woman took to the stage that was in the building just over the river, and started to sing.

'What is she saying?'

He translated for her. 'Going to test my voice, in a song,' he said. 'It is about a woman who is approaching a man to ask a question.'

'What question?'

'She has not said. She says she is a prisoner of his stare. Now she says she is going to drink alcohol. Like a ... *redentor*, what is the English word? A forgiving? A redeemer? I don't know. Then she is going to take his hand. Really just a funny little song. But it's OK.'

This could be the next step. The process did not apply here, she thought, while a running commentary of the lyrics came into her headset. *She says she will invent a ritual.* Establish a sense of urgency. Decide on the optimal course of action. *She is saying she will find a poem on the surface of her being.* In a near-deserted office in a city on the brink of erupting, before the call centres go dark, before there are machines to do both their jobs. Before all that happens, what else might. Turn your kind, welcoming face to mine. The song ended.

'You touch the statue every morning,' she heard herself say. 'I walk behind you and I see you do it. Why do you do it.'

She could hear him breathing into her ears. She reached forward for his shoulder. Before she made contact, a call came through.

'You're through to All Energy, this is Javier, how can I help you this evening?'

Someone was angry about the amount on their bill, claiming they were being ripped off, and what was he going to do about it.

'I will wait for you by the statue,' she said, and put her headset down.

She sat beside the statue on the bench. I can apply my own process, she thought. I can have fun. I can ask questions. I am not a prisoner. I can drink alcohol like a redeemer. I could walk with him through this city before I leave it. I could breathe into his ear. I could ask him to sing the song for me again, slowly.

She opened one of the cans she'd bought from the off-licence. She waited for a few minutes. How many are sufficient, she thought. He was stuck on calls, perhaps. Or his shift went until midnight, and she could not sit like an idiot for three hours. Or he had other things to do. He would not waste time meeting people he did not know and who were not staying. Or he knew she was there to destroy things, and his manager had warned him to say nothing to the robot consultant who was zero craic. It was ridiculous, she concluded. I do not drink beer on benches and make foolish proposals that would not meet approval or generate results. I have not saved him from oblivion. He does not owe me an explanation, or anything else.

I have never heard of you, she said to the iron face next to her. *Pouring redemption for me*, the inscription said. That is just a coincidence. Do not correlate, she thought. But maybe since you are a poet, maybe you have something on the surface of your being that could help. She put her hand around its shoulder. Do you know why a man from Portugal touches your shoulder each morning? Maybe he does it because he does not have to. Is that it? Maybe you remind him of someone. Maybe you make him think of his father. Maybe he is saying sorry to you, or it is good to see you again. Or I will never see you again.

She threw the half-drunk beer into the canal. She walked back towards the hotel. She passed the window of a pub, and looked up at the screen. It was the interval, and some kind of dancing show was on. A woman was moving, with her arms stiff by her side, bouncing on her heels. Then she stretched out her arms, as if to say, *I am not doing it that way anymore, this is the new process.* A man came in, his feet hammering the floor, the drums thundering in response. The man and woman circled each other, eyes and shoulders connected, moving as one. A line of people moved out of the darkness into the light to join them. They were moving up and down in unison, and more and more came, surging forward, as if they were all saying *look at us, look where we are going, we are all energy and you cannot stop us.* They all froze at once and the man and woman looked at each other. There was a roar from the crowd in the arena, matched by a roar in the pub, like in a football match when a goal is scored. We're going to win, it sounded like to her. A mass of people, an entirety, shouting the old way is gone, we are here, and we are going to win.

★

Her next visit to Dublin was fifteen years later. This time she had her own team, deployed to value a range of distressed assets and allocate them into a toxic bank based in a building not far from where she'd done her first solo assignment. She told her team over dinner about her first time in the city.

'I was very early in my career,' she said, 'Very naive, when it came to stakeholder management. This was when I was cutting my teeth on IVR projects. Simple stuff.'

'I can't imagine you as naive,' said the woman who she'd chosen from her award-winning Y2K team to run operations.

'The unions blocked it,' she told her. 'I wouldn't let it happen now.'

'I don't think they would have much say, these days,' another of her team said.

'No. But then – they were, it was the beginning, you know? Their confidence and their cranes were about to rise into the sky. Chicken rolls and deluxe apartments would soar in tandem.' Her team laughed and she drank in their respect. They were loyal and unquestioning. They would never dare ask her: what do you do for fun, when you are not working? There was so much to do. There had been relationships, there had been opportunities. But she was busy, she had to travel a lot, and if they couldn't understand priorities, that was their problem. Mutually exclusive.

'They were about to leverage themselves, deck themselves out in a manner to which they were not accustomed, buy apartments in Bulgaria, fly too close to the sun. I can pinpoint the moment it all started, actually,' she said to her team.

She thought back to that moment, looking in the pub window. She had seen the stage show, treating herself to a ticket on an assignment in New York, she had the DVD with the original cast and all of the increasingly disappointing spin-offs that followed after Flatley became misaligned. *The Lord of the Dance* was nowhere close, even Irish people had to admit the jig was up by then. And the show in New York was not the same as that first time. How could anything live up to what she'd seen through that window, and watched over and over on YouTube. *The interval that eclipsed the main performance*, as someone had commented.

'And it all came crashing down, of course,' one of her juniors said.

'As it always does. And then we pick up the pieces. I remember thinking ...' Maria said, and looked out the window of the restaurant, onto the canal. She could see the bench. She had met thousands of people since then. All putting up resistance, all eventually capitulating, quietly disappearing. The call centre building was apartments now. No chance he was still here. No line of inquiry she could pursue. She could walk over and sit by the statue, she thought. That old iron man is still there. But her team were keen to go on to a real Irish pub, and they were her responsibility, and she needed to ensure it was an early night.

'Remember thinking what?' one of them said.

'It doesn't matter. Now let's find a fun pub,' she said.

They cannot be kept back, is what she thought, looking in the window, at the end of that April fifteen years earlier, and at the start of what was to come. That was the thing about them. They would make their own rules, and then subvert them, and keep pushing forward until they fell, and then they'd say *ah well, it was fun while it lasted lads. We'll be back again.* Is that a better way to be, she had speculated. Break free and move unexpectedly. Unlock your body and be wild to consequence. Say things to strangers and await a response. That is not me, she had concluded that night. I focus on what I can control. I do not take risks. Let maddening queries go unresolved into an infinite queue. I will never connect or move like that with someone. She had called music to the surface but hadn't waited long enough to convert it into dance. It had gone back down into iron. The city would explode around that man on the bench, and he would sit and watch, arms folded, chained in unre-deemed thought forever.

She had looked to the sky, turning away from the pub window and the cheering people that night. In the year 2000 everything is set to fall, she had thought. They don't know what's coming. I will be prepared. Be ready for things to fail, to fall, to dance right past you. It could take six years or six minutes. It could take the span of a song. But one way or another, everything would happen, or absolutely nothing. And either way, who is to say what could be caused or prevented.

She had locked her arms tightly by her side, fifteen years ago, and walked along the canal.

FLASH FLOODS

BEFORE WE GOT BACK HERE, the Hoover and me, to the charred remains of the Venue, and before we averted a flood, I set my father on fire. Oh stop, we're not heathens, and this isn't some Old Testament tale. I'm being textbook dramatic. My father was already dead and his wishes at Barber and Sons Funeral Home and Crematorium (locally known as the Barb-e-queue) were clear. You might have heard about it, if Mid-West FM extends into your particular forlorn corner of the wild wet. *The death has been announced of Paul Hearst of Killuna, suddenly at his home at the age of fifty-eight. Paul would have been known to many of our listeners, he helped many in a time of need and will be sorely blah blah* here's Wham with 'Wake Me Up Before You Go-Go', which was close enough to the last thing he said to me. Three years on from when that song came out, and they're still banging it out on Mid-West. Right after his death announcement? He wouldn't have liked that. My father was many things but a fan of Wham was not one of them. *He sings too high for a man.* Always turned the radio down in the car when they played it. Rest of the time, that dial was not to be touched. Wednesday was the first time in many's the year he didn't tune in to the death notices, and he was the headliner. Would have infuriated him more than his son ever did.

I'm grieving, of course. I'm not a monster. I mean, in public at least. I do the needful. Put on the black suit shake hands sob show. But it isn't for him. I'm grieving for the premature death of me, nailed in with him, because I hadn't the balls to say no and go-go. *The drama on you, Gordo. You've notions beyond. You have a good business in the town and your father to thank. I'd kill to be in your position.* This is what they said to me in O'Malley's when I got down in my cups and bemoaned my professional and personal servitude to the now permanently late Paul Hearst. *Don't be disrespectful,* they'd say. The same people that gave him his mark, and mine. Marks being how you're known here. Your given name, that doesn't hold much ground. We'll take that off you and give you something more apt. Marks, nicknames, whatever you call them where you're from: they're answers to questions. Question being, what did you do to earn *that*. No cruelty like a well-aimed mark. Good luck shaking it off.

I wanted no starring role in my father's send-off. Grinding out platitudes in front of a stadium crowd? No thank you.

'Are you sure you don't want to say a few words,' Father McVerry asked when he called in to me to make the arrangements. 'It's just – I'm, well, sorry, quite new to the parish, and sorry but I didn't know your father well, and, sorry but the tradition would be for the, principal mourner, to—'

'You're grand,' I said. 'Just say he'll be missed. Or, whatever.'

'Alright. If you're – sorry, if you're sure.'

I suppose if you're a priest you can't go wrong saying sorry in every sentence but he could say whatever he liked today. I had nothing to add.

Father McVerry motored through some very generic farewells. *Paul was an upstanding member of our community, always had time for everyone, will be missed by all.* I sat in the front row trying to come up with a mark for the new padre. Something to use in the Four Provinces Utter Shambles of a Hotel and Bar at the afters. Father McVerry Sorry. Play for laughs, show them all I'm grand. Our Father of the Never-Ending Sorrows. At the end he said *If you want to walk behind the hearse we will be* and I heard a snort from somewhere behind me on *hearse.* Some marks will follow you down into the flames. Have to admit, if I'd been sitting somewhere else I would have done the same. The train of mourners passed me one by one. *Sorry about your father. Sorry about Poca now.* There was only one person I wanted to shake hands with. Maybe Jimmy the Hoover, previously known as James Dolan Junior, hadn't made it home. Maybe didn't want to deal with his mark, or anything else here, and I wouldn't blame him.

Two marks on my father, rolled into one: The Hearseman of the Apocalypse. Poca for short. Probably the town's finest work. To admire the craftsmanship of it, you had to break it down.

First: Paul Hearst was a Bad Driver. Not completely his fault. He got his licence in the amnesty when the government decided they'd just clear the backlog in one go. Good luck all you L-platers, just try to keep your eyes on the road and Christsake take it handy. Slow and steady was how he took it evermore. Get stuck behind him? May as well get out and walk. Funeral speeds even on the bog road, where everyone else lurched out of the hidden dips to gulp a mouthful of death for a second. He had two styles of parking. Some days he could not get enough of the kerb. He'd mount it in the big lunk of a

Ford like a black dog in heat. Get at least three wheels up on it, wedged within an inch of the shop window. People would stop to give his latest performance their marks. I'd sink down into the back seat but I could still hear them.

'Look at what Poca's managed today.'

'Maybe he thinks the butchers is a drive-thru, hey?'

Other days he was less frisky with the kerb. Downshift into pure tease. *I know I gave you the ride of your life yesterday, grinding my gears and going up and back on you, just how you like it. But today I'll keep my distance. I'll not come within six feet of you. Keep you wanting more tomorrow.* Strangers passing through the town would stop behind him. Maybe thinking he'd stalled, or there was something ahead they couldn't see. Then he'd get out and walk away. They'd have to pull into oncoming traffic to get around, rolling down the window to shout. He paid them no heed whatsoever.

'I have a licence like the rest of you,' he'd say, taking it out of its plastic sheath and holding it up like he was in the FBI.

'Yeah. For fire, flood and fucking awful parking.'

His attempts to teach me to drive were not our finest hours. He punched my arm every time I slipped out of gear or went too fast, which in his book was anything overtaking sheep velocity. *Do you want to end up in the ditch? Is that what you want? Do you have a death wish?*

James Dolan Senior, the Hoover's father, taught his son and me. *May as well teach you both at once*, he said. *And no disrespect to your father*, he said, *but — just so you, get a handle on . . . the basics.* That's fine with me Mister Dolan. I never told my Dad a word of it.

Me and Jimmy sat in the front and took turns doing the gears or steering. Between the two of us we could control a vehicle age of fifteen. We were best friends until we drove off in different directions. Him to London. Me keeping a tighter circle, round the bog roads, first with my father, then as he struggled, on my own. I'm still not great behind the wheel. Not that I've too much ground to cover anyway. Our work took in a fifty or so mile radius of the town. The assessment territory of Hearst and Son. As of today, just Son. Sole proprietor.

The work was the second part of my father's mark: Apocalypse Now. Or as soon as we arrived at our destination. Not quite fair to say death and destruction followed. We drove towards it. Slow and steady, mind. I cut my teeth on weekends and during the school holidays. Bit young for it, a mother might have said, if one had been there to say it. The only voice was his, pushing back the curtain. *Up and out. There's a job and you're coming with me. Get a taste of what men do when they're working. What else are you going to do. Lie in bed? Slide around the house on your own?* All sounded better options, but these were not discussions. We didn't have those. We were all business.

Usually flood or fire damage. I'd park the car, carefully, *Christ slow down*, then we'd get out and assess the wreckage. Stand with people in their hallways looking at water dripping down their walls. Stand in driveways, after fires, with people holding rescued family albums. Don't go back for anything, just get out: everyone knows this but no one listens. I was the photographer. Try to catch a water-stained wall or a burned-out hall in the best light. Dad would tell them it's just bricks and mortar. It can be fixed, rebuilt. Everything can be replaced. They let him say it, the ones in their loss, but they knew something was gone forever. He'd leave a respectful-ish gap before the pitch.

'You did the right thing to call us. We will assess the loss. Now, the insurance company won't want to pay out in full. It's in their interest to give you less than you're entitled to. They're hard to deal with if you don't know what you're doing. So let us do it. We'll get proper compensation.'

People are in a mess in that moment. If someone tells you they'll deal with it, sort it out, make the claim for you? Nine times out of ten, you've got a job. Take your cut. Throw in a little faux kindness to a man looking at his smouldering house.

'And if you need anything, sir. You are about the same size as myself. I have a suit I can give you. It's the least I can do.'

Assess the loss. Document the disaster. Drive a hard bargain with the insurer. Take your cut. A respectable (and profitable) service to the people of the town and surrounding bog body area. And on the way back from jobs he'd remind me of what a lifetime of honour and duty might entail. *This is a good business, Gordon. We help people out. Kind of thing now. Buck like yourself. Get into it and take it serious, and you're set up for life. I won't be at this forever. So.*

So being the question. *And Son* being the answer. It was etched in gold letters alongside his name on the office door when I was eighteen. School done, college not on the cards. *What else are you going to do, son?* Happy birthday, he said, handing me a set of keys to the office, an updated memorandum and articles of association listing me as a shareholder (forty-nine per cent, just to keep control), and a new camera. *I know you might have other ideas,* he said. *But Gordon. Most young lads never get the opportunity to co-own a business. You've a knack for it. Your mother would be proud,* he said. That was the start of my official journey, side by side, slow and steady, towards the next catastrophe. I didn't ask for it. I didn't have a better answer though. And this is how you end up seven years down the road, the worst option becoming the one and only, and now I'm one and only. *Hearst and Son: Loss Assessors. Fire Flood Property. Let us make your claim. Get what you deserve.* This was the poster outside the office. He let me put it up. It didn't also say: *Minus our ten per cent. Sometimes fifteen depending on the hassle factor and the validity of the claim. No arsonists need apply.* The small print is not what you hang on the wall.

We went past the office on our way to the Barb-e-queue to set him down. File a final report. A loss assessed and a claim on him, the one waiting for everyone, made good this morning. Today put no great feeling on me. I bear no ill will. What's the point in that? My bed was made and I lay down in it and that's that, except for the afters in the Four. Father Forgive Me politely declined. Probably had five communions and a bouncy castle to apologise to later.

Nobody took my Dad up on the suit offer, by the way. I'm wearing the notional spare today. It's too big for me. Black sleeves flopping, I've had to roll them up like I'm at a funeral afters on *Miami Vice.* It's just one day. Hang it at the back of the wardrobe later.

And now I'm sitting in the Four with a pint and coming towards me is the one person who I hoped, and dreaded, would show. I didn't know if word would reach him. Didn't see him at the church. And I doubt that the *Killuna*

People flies off the shelves of Piccadilly or that the World Service broadcasts the Mid-West death notices. It'd take a call to let Jimmy the Hoover know. *Your old friend Gordon's father, yes, you should come back.* His mother's job to inform him. I wasn't going to break the silence and ask. I was at his father's funeral a year ago, so fair's fair. Though I only had to walk three minutes from the office to attend. Me and Hoover didn't have much time for catching up that day. Big turnout. Quite the afters at the Four. I stood in a circle with him and various mourning freeloaders, but it wasn't exactly a chitter-chat moment and I wasn't pushing for it. That was the first time he'd been back since after the leaving cert. Decided to go-go to the land of Wham and Wembley and leave us all asleep while he set London alight, if you believe the goss and speculation. *I heard he drives a Roller. Big in construction. Penthouse on the river. Heard he got some London one up the duff and the mother is raging. Really? The Hoover? Sucks for him. Have you heard anything,* they asked me. *You must know. You were great pals.* That was years ago though. When we were boys. Don't confuse now and then. We're not in touch. Now we're two fatherless men at my Dad's funeral afters and he's walking towards me for, what exactly? Chat with his former co-pilot? Keep it general. Keep it cool.

'Hi Gordon.'

'Hi Jimmy. I didn't know you were—'

I saw him earlier coming out of the Barb-e-queue. I did know. I was bracing for this. Shake hands. What are you going to do. Hug? In the Four, in front of the assembled? Even at your father's funeral afters with your old friend Jimmy H that would not be the way. Good manly shake. There's been some mileage clocked up since we co-piloted his Dad's Corolla ten years ago. A bit of wear and tear. Holding up well enough though. Bit of a patch on top. Pale clearing in the forest. Same pattern as his father, no escaping.

'So, sorry, Gord. For—'

'Thanks. For, coming.'

'Sorry for your loss. Really am. Fifty-eight is a shocking age to—' he says.

'Yeah. Bad heart.'

'I know it's probably not fully ...'

'Uh, yeah. It's a lot to take in ...' I said.

'Yeah. When my Dad, it was, like weeks, before—'

'I'm sorry I didn't really get to talk to you at ... yours.'

This wasn't us. Twenty-five and talking like old ones. We could talk about anything, once. Now we're just banging out the coffin classics.

'I'd say you could do with another of those. If you – want company,' he said, pointing at my near empty glass.

'If you – I mean. If *you* want to.'

'Course, yeah.' He waved up to the bar. Are we going to settle in? To what? I ran away last time we met. I'm close enough to the door here, if another flash dash is necessary.

'So what's the – you're in – Brixton, still?' I ask him.

'Nah. Moved up to Fulham. Few years ago.'

'Oh right. Sorry Jimmy, it's been like, I don't know, how long since we—'

'Uh, James.'

'Sorry?'

'Meant to say. I go by James now.'

'Fair enough.'

I don't blame him. Go to London and get well clear of the mark. Take back your father's name now there's no grounds for confusion. Is there some deluded London love who doesn't know what you were. What you still are here. *Alright James darling? Pop down the local will we James? What's that? You're actually Jimmy the Hoover and they say you did what to what now? Cor blimey luv a duck let's keep it all hush hush.* Not so easy to shake it off here.

Someone slaps him on the back. A nobody town eejit who's such a nothing we never give him a mark. You had to earn them.

'Jimmy H, back from the bright lights.'

He shakes my hand. *Sorry now sorry Gordo.* But of course he wanted to talk to Lord James of London. I know my place. We were friends, but the ranking was clear. He was the star attraction. I stood in his light, but I was in his way. Let this lad cut in. Give Jimmy room. *How's London Jimmy / brilliant yeah / heard you're doing great there / doing alright now yeah / no cheeky cockney lady back with you / no man no / yeah sure keep your options open / hah yeah / yeah well listen see you again Hoov.*

Jimmy turns back to me, throwing his eyes up.

'You forgot to tell him you go by James now,' I said.

He laughs. 'I'm spreading the word slowly.'

'Do you remember his name?'

'No. Was hoping you'd help me out there.'

'Let's call him C-60.'

'Don't get it.'

'Blank tape.'

He has a good snort at that. Yeah, I'm still playing for laughs. That's two in the last few minutes. Second banana, wingman, comic relief: I don't know how else to play it. And you can rebrand yourself in Fulham all you want James Dolan Junior but you're Jimmy the Hoover here until you drop into the spot next to your

Dad. Not that he's heading that way soon. No, he's well enough preserved. Blue eyes on high beam. I can't see the bald spot up above if I look directly into them. Which I don't, for the record.

More drinks are dropped over. C-60 waves from the bar.

'Cheers now, 60,' Jimmy shouts back. 'Let's make that stick,' he says. Just to me.

'You used to give out digs when people said it in school. The, Hoover thing.'

'Yeah, well.'

'It was bullshit. Everyone knows,' I say. I asked him when it was going around. When we were fifteen. He wouldn't have lied. Not to me. I wanted to tell people it wasn't true. But once a mark is on, you wouldn't want to try and dispute the claim. Even if it's your best friend. Because you'll be marked next.

'It stuck, all the same,' he says. 'Everything sticks here.'

'You didn't.'

He shrugged.

James Dolan Junior on his baptismal cert. Jimmy to set him apart from his father. Until he was fifteen. The legend: One time his mother walked in on him when he was trying to pleasure himself with the vacuum cleaner. And she told her closest friend, and wildfire followed. The facts: No way. I know his mother. She wouldn't say something like that, to anyone, even if she saw it. And I know him. Or knew him. No way, right Jimmy? I mean, how would that even *work*? Some fucker just made it up, that's all it was. But it stuck. *There's Jimmy the Hoover,* people said, after a popular band at the time of his alleged domestic entanglements, unfortunately for him. Their song 'Tantalise' remains on the jukebox in O'Malley's by popular demand. Sometimes people called him Electrolux just to keep it fresh. He laughed it off, played along. *Yeah lads. I did it with the hoover. You should try it some time. I'll tell you which attachments work best.* Wise move. Just lean into your mark. If you can't take it, you better take off. Which in fairness, he did.

'London. Yeah. How's, it all ...' I ask him. Stay in the present. Don't look in the rear-view. Objects in the mirror can be closer than they appear.

'Yeah, good.'

'Construction, is it more, residential or—?'

'Commercial, mainly.'

'Good stuff.'

'And the, claims business. All good?'

'Yeah. Busy.'

And now we've kind of stalled. Look at us. Talking about work. This is how two boys turn into boring men, blank as C-60s. Old songs recorded over. In between the gaps on any tape, you can just about make out what was there before.

'My mother said you've been picking up on some jobs my Dad didn't quite, finish,' he says.

'The Tectite stuff. Yeah.'

'She said it was a right mess.'

'It's not great, no.'

I've been hoovering up his father's mess, and it's been pretty good for business, but I'm not going to say that. James Dolan Senior had bought a huge batch of cheap Tectite fittings in the north on one of his trips a few years before he died. *Price is great even in sterling,* he told us all in O'Malley's, *enough here to last me out.* They did outlast him, but not for long. It was a bad batch. Brought in from China. No disrespect to their manufacturing skills or Jimmy's father but these fittings were not built for the ages. Tectite joints are not supposed to fail. Not within the first ten years anyway. You probably have them in your house. They're holding your pipework together. I hope James Dolan Senior wasn't your plumber in his twilight years. When one cracks, which it will, your whole system is going to go. You'll wake up one morning with your boiler fried, water coming up through the floorboards and down the walls. And you'll call the plumber, and be told he passed away, but his widow will send someone. And you'll wonder if the insurance will cover it. And then, well, you know who to call.

I was following this trail of devastation around. One by one, the calls were coming in from new builds and refurbs and community halls. Break it to them on arrival. There was a bad batch of Tectite. Came in through the north. Did James Dolan ... that explains it. Unsuitable fittings are solid grounds for a hefty claim. Not against the dead, no point in that. Let me sort it for you, I tell them. I survey the damage and write the report, pass the claim to the insurer, who goes after the supplier in Newry, who lays it off on the distributor in Newcastle and back along the blame chain to a factory owner in Shenyang. Might take a year before there's a payout. You can't lose heart, I tell my clients. It will come good. Don't give up hope. I'll fight for you.

'Sorry James. It's nothing against your father.' But botch jobs need to be dealt with.

'It is a bit,' he says, fixing the blue beams on me. 'People calling my mother up, cursing him.'

'He wasn't to know.'

'He should have had more cop on. I told him, cheap parts are not worth it. But, you know what he was like.' Loved a bargain did James Dolan Senior. Pay the price in the long run.

'I know it's, not good for your mother. But, she gets the repair cost off the insur—'

'I'm in the trade, Gordon. I know how a claim works. Tidy enough business for you, though, I'd say.'

'I'm just – I'm trying to help her.'

'Yeah. Well. I'll be doing that from now on.'

'Doing what?'

'Any jobs that need fixing. Call me, not her.'

'How, you're over in—'

'I'm going to stick around here for a bit. She needs the help. With the backlog.'

She really does. *Another Tectite job Mrs Dolan. You'll need to send someone. Oh Jesus Gordon. Will this ever end.* Some little boy is dispatched and he's probably making it worse. I drove the rest of those bad bastard fittings to the dump for her. I sign off on the repair work for the claim. She's out of her mind with it. She really should just sell the business. But families tend to get mangled in these things, and it's carrying some debt. And now apparently Jimmy's here to deal with it. Which is not completely bad news. Depending on how he deals with it.

'I could show you one of them. So you get a handle on it. I've four next week,' I say.

'I know how to replace a Tectite fitting.'

'I have to sign off on it though. For the claim.'

'You don't have to be there, though. When I'm, working.'

He's looking down at his empty glass. It's true. I don't have to be there, getting in his way. I just thought, trying to be helpful. Smooth it over. I know these people and he doesn't. They get wind it's the son of the father who botched it, the wrong type of person might get into it with him. But no. Stay out of his light. He knows how to deal with it.

'I'll – I didn't mean, I know you know what to do.'

'Yeah. Sorry, Gordo. Just. People going on like my Dad did them over, I can't ...'

'I've never heard anyone say a bad word about him.' That's not true but he takes it.

'I – look. Let's not, talk about work. I shouldn't have, at your Dad's ...' he says.

'It's fine. Whatever's on your mind. It's fine.'

Don't stress it Jimmy. We are just a couple of lads having a business discussion, catching up, sort of talking about each other's recently deceased, and what they've left us both with. No big deal at all. I go up to the bar for us.

Risk of this is someone's going to come over and take my seat. Everyone here wants to talk to him. *Tell us about the Roller. Is it true about the penthouse. Who's the lady.* He was, still is, one of those people that a circle just forms around. I'd say you've had one in your circle too. The one who was just unquestionably, effortlessly, I mean fall-out-of-bed cool. Better hair, better records, better at pool, just – better. Without a word of self-praise or awareness. Which made him even cooler. Better house. His Dad was always up to the north for plumbing supplies and brought back the stuff of dreams. A Commodore 64. A portable TV. These things were in his *room*. I don't know how I became the one he let in. Maybe I was just no threat. Maybe he knew I needed it. Maybe he needed it too. Someone always has to be the one amazed, looking, wondering how you get to be like this.

I'd go to his house after school to do homework but really to play on the 64 and listen to records. We'd play *Daley Thompson's Decathlon* together. They didn't figure that two kids could beat any contender if they just pounded on the keyboard at the same time. Play games, listen to records, talk about them. We were obsessed. At least, I was. Go through the charts. *Can't believe Blondie dropped five places.* We liked pop. This has stuck with me. Give me a three-minute pop song any day over some miserable country dirge or some oh-so-serious men wearing trenchcoats in the snow. Tape them off the radio, holding the pause button on his ghetto blaster. Wait. Wait. Stop *talking*, Larry Gogan. And now he's left us all in the dust. To dust you shall not return, Jimmy. You're not made of ashes. You're something else completely. You're back, and that's something. But you're only here to fix a few busted joints, be a good son, and then you'll be gone again.

Someone taps me on the shoulder at the bar.

'Sorry about your father, now.'

'Thanks Eoiny.' Eoiny the lonely. Wears Roy Orbison shades on account of the glaucoma and has the build. He came custom-made for his mark. Only one in the town who actually introduces himself with it. Well, if it suits, wear it.

'No age to go. Hard enough now on you I'd say.'

'I'm alright. Thanks, though.'

'He was quick enough in going.'

'For once.'

'Ah here, I wasn't – saying anything about. I had a lot of time for the Hearseman, I mean, for your father.'

'You're grand.' I'd say you were the source of the church snort earlier, Lonely. I can make the jokes if I want. I could add in a few more doing the rounds. *Probably claimed back on the coffin for fire damage. Wonder he didn't scuff the side on the way in.* It's fine. I'll join in. I can show a mark of disrespect if I want. He put me here and held me here and before you say get over yourself, you could have gone to London or anywhere, what was stopping you – try it sometime when your name is on the door and someone needs looking after and see how easy it is to take off. See how easy it was for some, though.

'And the Hoover's back I see,' Lonely says, looking over. 'You two were the great pals.'

'Ah, long time ago.'

'He'd want to sort out his poor mother. She's in no position to take on his Dad's – I mean, he was a good man. But a fuckin' awful plumber.'

'Yeah, well. I think James is going to be helping his mother out.'

'James?'

'He's – going by that, now.'

'That's London for you.'

I happen to know, Eoiny, that you have those bad bastard Tectites in your little shit-box rental apartment out the Quarry road. I could tell you what's in store, but let's just wait until your tenants are flooded out and howling at their oh-so-shady landlord, and you can give me a bell then.

'Let me get you … what will you have,' he says, waving the barman over.

'It's fine, I'll get—'

'Come on Flash. Let me get you and the Hoov a couple of shorts. For the lads.'

Yeah. Flash. My mark. As in, well obviously. After Gordon Lightfoot according to my mother. Good strong name, she said. That's as maybe but it was a gift on a marker's plate. Flash as in the camera. The one I got for my eighteenth that I used for damage assessments. I took a lot of pictures around the town. Flash for wearing a yellow shirt to the Venue, one time. A present from a well-meaning, maybe perceptive, definitely demented aunt. But that just doubled down on the mark. I've heard them all. Go on, tell me I'm alive, morning after a big night. Tell me I've fourteen hours to save the world. I'll say what's the rush, so. I've heard Lightfoot used for me too. Flash for running all the way home from the Venue. One night. Lightfoot for go fuck yourself, Eoiny.

I went back to James, definitely not Jimmy, with pints and two shorts, courtesy of the Big O.

'Lonely sends his regards,' I said, setting down the doubles.

'State of him,' he said, raising his glass to him smiling at us from the bar. 'Man needs to take a good look at himself.'

'I never called you that, by the way.' In case he's forgotten, I never said it to him. Let's not be all business here.

'What.'

'Jimmy the, whatever.'

'I don't care. But, well, thanks like.'

I do a little bow. Not sure what I'm playing at here. I'm slipping a bit off the perch now. But it's never just now, is it. Everything is leaching up out of the floor-boards. Go down and look at the damage.

'You punched Pat Mahoney in the face for saying it. In the Venue. Right in the middle of 'Come on Eileen'. Results night,' I say.

'I don't remember that.'

'Well. I don't either. Not really. I was outside. Just, that was the story. Anyway.'

'I had a load of cans that night. And I punched a lot of people for saying it. So could be you're right.' He takes a swig of the whiskey and looks off to the side. Means what. No more about that?

Course he remembers. Leaving cert results. Epic night guaranteed. All of us in the Venue, three miles outside the town along a dirt road. Maybe to keep the noise away from the good people trying to sleep. Or let people get into trouble in the dark and pretend you didn't see. The Venue dance floor was the size of a small sitting room. You had to take turns, or all pile in heaving if one of the big songs came on. 'Come on Eileen' was one of them. Pat Mahoney had to go and do the whoosh noise and sing *Come on Jimmy, Oh I swear you're sucking*. That is the story as it's told anyway. I wasn't there, as I said. I was outside. Official town record is that Pat said that and Jimmy just lost it and decked him and he had it coming. Part true but not quite a full account.

'Pat Mahoney. Now there was a prick,' Jimmy says.

'In Australia now.'

'Is he yeah. I don't really – keep up with, all this,' he says, flicking a wrist at the grief junkies making short work of the damp sandwiches and the small amount I've put behind the bar.

'You're not missing much.'

'Well. I'll be around for a bit. Until these fucking fittings are dealt with.'

'Maybe Eoiny there can burn through them with his laser eyes,' I say. Point at someone else and have a laugh. Best form of attack and defence. 'Can you imagine him up a ladder?'

'You would have some claim if he fell on you,' he says, laughing, and goes off for a slash.

See this is more like it. Like when we were boys. Just messing. We're not fucking sad old men like Eoiny. He was a sad old man back then, at the bar that night in the Venue. There's always one, just a little too old to be hanging with the young ones. That's all we were in the Venue. Boys shotgunning cans, shooting looks at girls, in the dark with no idea. Jimmy could have had any number of shots. Girls were always into him. He paid them no heed and that drove them mad. *I could not be bothered*, he said. *Not with the likes of them anyway.* Yeah wasting our time, I said that night. Not *our* time. They weren't looking at me. Didn't matter if I wore a yellow shirt and a neon sign on my head, they'd look past the banana and focus on the brighter light in the Venue. *Couldn't care less*, he'd say. We'd make fun of them. Just skitting whispering like. Not cruel stuff. I mean no more than anyone. Eoiny saw us that night, giggling. Maybe I was leaning into Jimmy, saying something in his ear. I saw Eoiny talking to Pat. Pat came up to me on the dance floor.

'You'd want to give Jimmy some room to breathe there Flash.' He was shouting into my ear the way you had to in the Venue. Saying something private at the top of your lungs into a cupped ear.

'What are you talking about.'

'No girl can get near him. The way you are.'

'What way. What's your problem?' I said.

'Are you in love with him or something?'

'Fuck off,' I said. 'Fuck right off.'

'Everyone knows. It's obvious. Why don't you leave him alone, Lightfoot.'

I did. Immediately. Get the fuck away from this. Pushed out through the crowd. Leaned up against the breeze block wall in the cark park. This was in on me. This was out. They were all saying it. Fucking obvious.

Jimmy came after me. I knew he wouldn't let me leave the circle. He was my best friend. And now look.

'What happened. Why did you run off,' he said.

'Nothing. Just needed some air.'

'What did he say to you. Pat.'

'Nothing. It's – just leave it.'

'Gord. Just tell me.'

I said it. To the concrete car park. I couldn't look at him. Should have left it. But I couldn't.

'Right. Right,' he said, and walked back in. I remember thinking, this is all going to rip now. Someone is going to get told very clearly what is what. And what is not. Someone is going to get hurt. I leaned up against the breeze block wall. Jimmy came back out a few minutes later, flexing his shoulders up and down, shaking his head.

'That's dealt with,' he said. He lit a cigarette, and offered me one. I tried to put it to my mouth but my hands were shaking. He took it, lit it, dragged to get it going, and passed it back.

'Jimmy,' I started.

'I said it's dealt with.'

'I don't know if it is.'

He didn't say anything.

I'm sorry, I could have said. After I tried. I could have said, then or the next day, I'm sorry and I'd had a fill of drink and I'm sorry if I got the wrong idea just forget it, forget it, leave it. But I'd wanted to ask for so long. Am I in the dark. Am I out of my mind. I have to let it out.

'Don't,' he said, when I tried. 'That's not. I'm not. Fucksake man?'

I turned, threw up and ran. Knocked into Eoiny at the gate and kept running. Whatever he thought he saw, whatever I thought was slowly burning, all gone in a Flash. Eoiny saw. And burned a new mark on me.

I couldn't call over to him the next day. And say what. *Lot of drink last night Jimmy, don't even remember.* Or, *it was nothing, just, messing, obviously, fuck Pat, I don't.* Or, *I mean of course I do, you're my best friend. I just thought. I didn't know if.* Yeah, try sucking those words out of yourself at seventeen. Or just shut up and hide in your room. Fix the leak and concrete over it.

He didn't come looking for an explanation, or to punch my lights out, or anything else that would have been a fair claim. We dodged each other the rest of the summer. I had a load of his records. But I wasn't going over to his to have a break-up. Let it slip away. Run and don't look back.

He went to London that September. I went to work and kept my head down. Stick to something you can deal with. Assess damage, make a claim for it. Fix what's obviously broken. Tend to your own damage in silence. Tend towards nobody and nothing. Pretend it never happened, go for pints, nobody says it to your face, but you know they know. You're going to crack, and they're waiting. They beat you, or worse, this lad said to me one time when we were doing nothing, nothing, just walking down by the quarry. *Some lad in Dublin was left for dead. There are places you can go but there are people watching and they know where you live. I can't,* he said. *You're marking yourself for death.* Jesus Christ we were only out for a walk. I didn't even especially like him. It was more I just wanted to say I am here, you're not alone, please say it back. I didn't even have the balls to say that. That's how you become the one at the bar, too old for dancing, too alone for your own good. Isn't it, Lonely. I see you too. Both of us marked, burning in silence.

'I still have a load of records belonging to you,' I say to Jimmy when he sits back down.

'Oh, yeah. Well. Statute of limitations, I think you can keep them.' Statute expired? I don't know. Seems like the day for it.

'And your, our tapes. Remember when we used to—'

'Yeah. Sorry, I should have, called over. Before I, left,' he says.

'Nah, it was – I was busy anyway, with Dad.'

'Yeah.'

'I missed you though. It's OK, to say that. Isn't it?' Tell me you see me. Don't look past me again.

'Yeah. Course. I – look. It was all, just—'

'Do you want to get out of here. Get some air? Go for a drive, or something.' Let me today. Let me say what I want.

'Uh, I've had a few pints, so—'

'Please?' I say. 'I've just. I've had enough of all the – you know?' Enough of all the sorrys are you alright. Can we just get out of here.

He's a good driver. Right amount of confidence and daring. We're along the bog road, the town behind us. He's picking up speed. Over the limit in every sense.

Letting someone drive is a phenomenal act of faith. A foot away from me he holds my life in his hands. Eyes on the road now Jamesy. Keep her ticking over.

'I'm really sorry about your Dad,' I say to him. 'He was always very good to me.'

'Remember when he taught us both to drive?'

'Yeah. You at the wheel and me changing gears. Co-pilots. Like when we used to play *Daley Thompson's* on your 64.'

'We wrecked that keyboard.'

'I could make a claim,' I say and he laughs. I'm still gas, aren't I Jimmy. I'm still here, still playing for laughs.

'Always working, Gordo. Your parents would be proud.'

'Not sure about that.'

All those hours in his house. Those were around the time my mother died. Is that why he let me in. Let me out of that house where it was just me and my father, too full and too empty. *She's irreplaceable, your mother. I could never.* A word that was reserved in our line of work for high value items that would drive up a claim. Family heirlooms, of deep sentimental value. Irreplaceable means this is going to cost you. But for her, it meant what it meant.

'I don't think my mother would be proud of me at all,' I say as he swerves around the corner.

'You can't say that.'

I look out the window. I think about what she would have said, if she was a ghost in the back seat. *What the hell are you doing, Gordon. Would you not go off and make something of yourself. Are you just going to be that little boy, the replacement fixture in your father's chair, until your heart gives out like his. Because your pipework is inherited. You'll feel it in your chest, one day as you file a report, and the last thought will be: I didn't become myself. I became him. And that's your problem, son. Nobody's to blame but you.*

'I think my mother would have told me to get the fuck out of here long ago.'

'Still an option,' Jimmy says.

'There's – work. Not that easy. I'm in the middle of all these claims.'

He pulls off the road. Back down the track we go.

We're leaning against the low breeze block wall again, looking at the blackened skeleton of the Venue. Charred sign hanging on an angle. He's taken out a hip flask and I'm here again with a fill of drink and what else in me.

'State of this place,' he says, kicking a stone across the car park.

'Yeah. I mean. It was never great.'

'Can't believe Mallin torched his own place.' Yeah. Not all claims are valid.

'He was a chancer.'

'I heard you and your Dad caught him out.'

'There's always a sign. Burn pattern in the upstairs stockroom. Too even. Lighter fluid. Same pattern in the bar.'

'Fucking idiot.'

'If he'd just done the bar, he might have got away with it. Fire burns up, not down. People tend to over-engineer their frauds.'

I'm doing it again. I'm trying to show him. Look. I know things. I'm good at this. I'm not saying I'm great. I'm not like you. But this is my job. I'll make a fair claim and get what I can. But you won't get away with a cover-up. There's always a sign. My Dad was the expert.

Discover the incriminating evidence. Set it out clearly to the accused. *What's wrong with you. You can't do this. You're a disgrace. You will end up in jail. Or worse.*

'You know your stuff,' Jimmy is saying.

'Been around it a good while now.'

He lights a cigarette. My hands are OK this time.

'Fucking shithole place. I never liked it,' he says.

'No. We never had a good night, here.'

He looks straight ahead.

'What you did. Here. That time.'

Don't look at me. Please don't look at me now.

'Freaked me out Gordon.'

'I know. I'm – I think about it all the – I'm sorry. I had no ...'

'No. It's – I just. I'm fine with. I've no bother, with ... I mean. I live in London yeah? But, I'm not ...'

'Yeah. No, I know.' I know. Same as I always knew, same as my mother and my aunt did. Say nothing. Stay in the dark and die alone. That's the road ahead.

'But like. I'm saying. Whatever you – that's fine. With me. I'm saying.'

'OK. Yeah. Well, thanks for. Saying that.'

Don't throw up again. Don't start crying. Don't do any of that. Man up.

'Fucksake man, what is this,' he says, and hugs me. 'It's just us.'

Hold him very lightly. Don't think. This isn't. Let it end. Let him go.

'Thanks. By the way,' I say. 'For um. Fighting for me. That night. If that's the right ...'

'You didn't need me to fight for you. You were always pretty cool when it came to things like that.'

'Um, cool I was not.'

'Yeah you were. Hanging back. You were funny. Funnier than me. You were the one who knew what was going on.' That doesn't sound like me, at all, but take it. Take a compliment from the one who knows you best.

'Let's just go with thanks for knocking out Pat Mahoney.'

'It was my absolute pleasure,' he says. He passes his flask and I take a swig. Breathe. You are not dying. No more than anyone. Breathe.

'So that's – dealt with,' he says, again.

'Yeah. It is.'

There's something else I want to put to him though. If we're going to deal with things. May have been his pleasure but I want to be strictly business. Sometimes I have an idea that's not completely wrong.

'Can I say something. Not about – that. About, the Tectite stuff.'

'You want to talk about fittings? Now?'

'All the jobs your Dad used them on. He would have kept records.'

'I mean, records would be stretching it. But, yeah. It's all in a pile.'

'So, strictly it's on the owner to call the insurance company when there's damage. And if they need a loss assessment they'll call me.'

'Yeah. So?'

'I was thinking. We could just. Deal with it.'

'Deal with what.'

'We tell the people with the bad fittings. There's something that's going to go wrong. Might already be gone and they can't see it. And we'll fix it. Get ahead of it.'

'That's – no. It doesn't work that way.'

'It could.'

'We don't know which ones are actually going to fail. People would think we're scamming them. We could end up fixing things that aren't broken.'

'We wouldn't be. They're all going to crack, sooner rather than later. You know they are.'

'But then, there's no – loss? How's that good for you?'

'It's not. It's really bad, for business. They can't claim for preventative measures. I'd get nothing. You could charge for, maintenance or something. But I'd get nothing.'

'Why would you do that?'

'I don't know. Just. Thought it'd be good to, clear it all up. Then, nobody is thinking bad about, your Dad or I don't know. Me. When it goes wrong.' Just for once, deal with things before it all goes to shit.

'My Dad wasn't – he wasn't bad.'

'I know. Nor was mine. Just, doing their jobs.'

He flicks his cigarette into the car park. 'Save the world and they'll never know to thank you. This is textbook Flash Gordon.'

'Why don't we try. Just with one. I know of one, for sure. We could go over there now,' I say.

'Uh, we're a little drunk? And you're in, funeral gear.'

'Yeah. Still though. Day that's in it?'

Eoiny shit-hovel rental. Fuck him anyway but he's a useful test case. We told the women living there that Eoin had sent us to do a routine check on the heating system. They said they were already noticing some damp spots. They'd called him twice and he hadn't come back. Well, we're here to fix it, I said. Simple job. Three fixings needed swapping out. He had the parts in the car. I knew enough to be helpful. Seen enough botch jobs to learn from them. *You hold the pipe there and I'll swap it out*, he said. It's a quick enough fix if you know what you're doing. We did.

'That will save you a lot of heartbreak,' I said to the woman at the door, and maybe I'm swaying a bit but she had the good grace to say nothing.

'Thank you, very much,' she said. 'Do I – sorry about the, cost of—'

'There's no charge,' I said. 'We'll talk to Eoin. Let him know what we fixed.'

'You're great lads,' she said.

I don't know. We're just doing a favour. For each other and for whoever. We're neither of us on the make. Just putting some things right. That's our business.

'That felt – good,' he says as we go back to the car.

We're back in the town and he's pulled up outside my office. Another swig of the hip flask. We've stalled now. Just say something. Cap this day off with something to look forward to.

'So,' I say, turning to him, 'What do you think. About, fixing the rest of them.'

'I'll do it,' he says. 'Let's make a list and go through them all. Together.'

'I'd like that.'

'But there are terms and conditions.'

'I'm good with paperwork,' I say. But he's not messing.

'Once it's done, I'm going back to London.'

'Yeah. Obviously.' I know this is just a few weeks. Month at best. That's ok. That's good enough.

'And you're coming back with me.'

'Not that easy, James. I've – responsibilities here.'

'Close up shop. For a while.'

'There's, outstanding claims. I can't just—'

'Compassionate leave. Give yourself that.'

'I'm not really – I'm actually, fine.'

'Sure. But just, do it anyway. Give yourself a few weeks. Or as long as you want.'

'To do what?'

'To see. What's over there. For you.'

'I don't know anyone there except you.'

'So? You'll stay with me. And then decide, if you want to come back to – this,' he says, pointing a thumb at the office door. 'But, if you'll. Just hear me. I know you. I still, know you.'

'I know you do.' Like nobody ever has.

'And I know that whatever it is you want, Gordo. In your, life. It's not here.'

I could laugh it off. Ah here Jimmy, my life's not that bad. London's not for everyone. And it's alright for you but I can't just go. You don't have to fix everything, you know. Make light of it. Tell more lies. But. There's a crack in my head and he's shouting into it. As loud as Pat Mahoney's voice in my ear on the dance floor.

'I'll – thanks, James. I'll definitely ... think about it.'

'No. Just do it. That's the deal. Take it or leave it.'

'Can we talk about it in the morning? I'm – it's been, a lot. Today. I'm wrecked.'

'I'll pick you up at nine,' he says. 'And bring one of those old tapes, for the car.'

I get out and steady myself. I tap the roof twice and he's off. And, for once, I'm looking forward to work in the morning. Tomorrow I'll slide in beside my best friend. We'll slip back into it. He'll remember how it went. You can block out everything, you can try and silence the mind, but pop songs, great ones: they're hard wired in. Switch to the radio and catch up on the latest. Mid-West keep playing 'Take On Me'. I'll sing along too high, well out of my range. He'll laugh at that and I'll look over at him, cigarette dangling from his lip. He won't leave me hanging. He'll join me up there. Is that the deal I'm doing?

I've my keys in my hand and I'm looking at the sign on the door, etched into the frosted glass, as my swaying reflection looks back at me. A blank black shadow. Be nameless in London. Take on a new shape. Do I have that in me? All you have is your name, Dad said. Let it stand for something.

My key is on it now. Deface and face yourself. It's just letters. It's not a sentence. It's not a crime. Remove some marks and make a new one. The gold flakes away easy.

Hearst And Son

Hear A Son

Hear me, James Dolan Junior, come back to assess the damage. What you heard, one way or the other, in a Venue long gone. What I couldn't say: I meant it. Don't worry. I won't try to say it again. Not to you. Maybe I'll say it to someone else, someday. I might hear it back. What you said tonight. That was enough for now.

Keep going. Cut into it.

Hear

Hear this too. Broadcast it on Mid-West, put it in the *People*. Business for sale in Killuna. A good one. But not for me. I'm done with losses. Scrape away what I am no longer.

He

Let that stand. He is a going concern. Where he goes is my business.

Maybe we'll pilot the Corolla together tomorrow, like we used to. But it's high time I took the wheel. Assess what's left. Write off what's lost. Drive out of the ditch and the dark, into myself.

THE LEASH

HE PULLS TOO HARD. YOU wrap the leash twice round your hand to bind him tight to your heel. You should school it out of him, this raw energy for the world, but it seems cruel to contain it. Why not let him run wild instead of tethering and taming? Every blade of grass a lush specimen to be savoured. Every hound he encounters the most delectable creature, and fair game. What if each of us was so enraptured at the sight of another? We'd all be constantly in bits. No wonder he's conked out most of the time. And this is post-neutering. On which a two-for-one daddy-doggy deal was mooted by Susan and the second part is still a live discussion. You let him pull you on. He knows where you're headed. Let his will pull you there.

You didn't want to get one. You made your case at the kitchen table.

'It's a lot of responsibility,' you said. 'What if we go away? Who would mind it?'

'Stall on the clichés,' Susan said. She has no problem clarifying authority levels at home. Ranking ahead of you were her, your daughter Ella, and a currently theoretical dog.

'What if it has mental issues from a difficult past?' you tried. 'They can bite you out of nowhere.'

'What if you have mental issues,' Ella said.

'What if it gets sick and dies and you have to deal with death, Ella?'

'She knows what death is, she's eleven and she's not stupid,' said Susan.

'We'll see who's taking it on a walk when it's freezing and raining and dark,' you said.

'We sure will,' said Ella.

'Well, I've made my views clear,' you said. You say that a lot. But the noise it makes is less like a definitive pronouncement and more like the dishwasher: an irritating hum that your cohabitants are initially aware of, but which quickly subsides into the background. Part of the tedious household machinery. They let it run while they go about their business and there's a welcome silence when the cycle ends and you go back on standby.

'Well, that's all decided. Now pick one,' Susan said, handing you the computer.

You scrolled through rows of plaintive puppy eyes. All asking if you'd be their best friend, if you'd let them sit at your feet, if you'd take care of them in return for a lifetime of loyalty and unconditional love. You looked at the row of human eyes on you in the kitchen, asking none of those questions and proposing no such arrangement.

'What about this one?' you said, pointing to a pointer or setter or something like that. You didn't know dogs. Not then anyway. 'He looks like he wouldn't be any trouble.'

'That's the wrong one,' said Ella. 'It's this one.'

She pointed to a ball of fluff with a bow in its hair. You could already hear the yippy little shit. You could already see her regarding you disdainfully as someone there to provide food and toys and otherwise stay well out of her way. You already had a full complement of those.

'Why did you ask me if you've already decided?'

'We thought it might make you give in faster,' Ella said.

But you chose a different one when you were dispatched for pickup. A rejected guide dog. They didn't say rejected. They said *available for rehoming*. He was too curious for the job, the man said. Kept looking around and wandering off. Could pull someone into traffic if he saw a nice leaf in the road. But otherwise he's a grand lad, you were assured.

Black lab. Proper-looking dog. One you wouldn't be ashamed to have on a leash. Not much in the way of cute about him admittedly and not a puppy and you had been warned not to veer off mission: fluffball or bust. But something in the way he looked at you. Something in the longing. *If you don't pick me, nobody will.* And that line of appeal just goes straight into you, doesn't it? So you used your executive authority. Unwisely.

Down the wide road then along the edge of the park. You have established a routine, the two of you. You know what you're looking for, as you both push along. A sign of life. Any second now she'll come towards you, her little dog in tow. You will watch her approach. And at the corner, at the now usual time and place, all four of your paths will cross.

Overcurious non-guider didn't land well back at base.

'You were supposed to get the other one,' Ella said as you spun out his backstory.

'Size of him. Where's he supposed to fit?' asked Susan, pushing him down off her jeans.

You all looked to him for an answer. He seemed to be the only one pleased to be there, knocking homework off the coffee table with his tail.

'He'll fit in fine. Come on guys. Doesn't he deserve a second chance? Shake off his past and start again?' you said.

'He's not in witness protection,' Susan said. 'And what do you really know about him? What if he's not quite the hard-luck story? Remember, mental issues? Biting us out of nowhere?'

'Then I will feel bad about my decision,' you said.

'I wanted the fluffy one,' said Ella.

'Someone took that one. And this one we can take out for walks right away. Puppies are really boring, Ella. They don't tell you that on the website. They don't do anything. They just lie around and sleep. Like babies.'

'So now you hate puppies *and* babies?'

'Let's just focus on welcoming our new friend, will we?'

'So what are we going to call him. If he's ... staying,' asked Susan.

'He has a name already, actually.'

They looked at you.

'Billy,' you called.

Billy looked up at the sound of his name. As it turned out, for the last time.

'That's a stupid name,' Ella said.

'I think it's a good name,' you said in his and your defence. 'Good strong name. And it really suits his—'

'Let's call him Lookie,' said Ella.

'Lucky?'

'No, *Lookie*. Because he looked at too many things and got fired.'

'Ella, that is brilliant,' said Susan.

'You can't just, change, someone's ...'

'Here Lookie,' she said, pulling him towards her by the collar.

The dog that was briefly Billy looked up at you. *So it's you and me against these two, that how it's going to be?*

Along the road towards the usual spot. It's getting harder to keep this going. You have tells like anyone does.

'I'll take him out,' you said in the hall, making your move last night. It was that part of the day where you don't fit. Homework is half done, dinner is on, you're surplus to requirements. And you've got to get out.

'I took him out earlier,' Susan said.

'Well, I'll take him again,' you said. 'Just get some air.'

'Take Ella with you,' said Susan.

'Ah, no. She won't want to. I don't mind. By the time I ask her and she gets her shoes and her coat, you know ... yourself.'

'What's your route?' she asked as you put on the leash.

'Oh you know. Just down and around.'

'Down and around. Right.'

She gives you a look. Just enough. She has an imagination. So do you. And she knows you do.

Six weeks since this started. She was walking towards you with her dog. And what's not normal about that? Who are you, just two people out with their dogs? Absolutely so what. The dogs pulled towards each other. And as two responsible owners, you let them have a moment. They wasted no time getting familiar.

'Sorry, he's a bit ...' you said.

'Oh, so is she,' she replied.

You both looked down as the mutual examination played out, until you felt like you were standing next to a stranger at a five-dollar peep show. Some kind of conversation had to ensue. That's just natural.

'What's his name?' she asked.

'Eh, Lookie.'

'Lucky?'

'Yeah.'

Because you couldn't be bothered. You were just over the weeks of reprogramming to get him to answer to the new stupid name. You could have said Billy. Sometimes you still do when nobody is around to monitor. When you do he bounces up on you. *You remember! I knew I wasn't going mad! Who the fuck's Lookie?*

'And this is ...?' you asked, pointing down towards the indecency unfolding at your feet.

'This is Luna.'

One of those stupid fluffy ones you'd narrowly avoided, with an idiotic name to match. In another life this could be your situation. You made the right call. And yes the requested pup was available when you went that day. But nobody needs to know that.

'Well, Look ... Lucky, meet Luna. Although I think you're well past pleasantries,' you said.

She laughed. Three little hees in descending register. Here, this is for you. Lap it up.

And on she went with a *see ya*. That could have been that. But after a distance, you turned, to look again. She was looking when you turned around. She started it.

You timed it the same the next evening. Same route. Slowed down a bit on the road. Chance you'd see her again or a one-off? There she was, coming towards you. The dogs were delighted to pick up where they'd left off.

'You going this way?' she asked, cocking her head down the road in the wrong direction.

You weren't, but you were now. It was going to add a bit of time and mileage but you didn't mind. Definitely didn't mind.

On the second walk, human names were exchanged and a nice, easy conversation about what good companions dogs could be.

'She keeps me company,' she said. Company. Means no one else? Means everything else?

'So where did you get Lucky?'

'I have a confession, actually. His name isn't Lucky. It's Lookie.'

'Lookie?'

'Yeah. With two *o*s. As in, look at me.' She did. 'He was supposed to be a guide dog but he had a wandering eye and wasn't fit for the job.'

'Poor boy. Dismissed.'

'Well, rehomed, yeah.'

'He must love that you remind him of his disgrace every time you call him.'

'He used to be called Billy,' you said. Your poor confused dog looked up. 'But it got, changed.'

'He looks more like a Billy to me,' she said.

'I know. Doesn't he? That's what *I* said.'

'But I guess you need to stick with the new moniker now.'

Susan would never say moniker. If you said moniker she'd say what's wrong with saying name. This wasn't Susan though, was it? It very much wasn't.

'Well LuckyBillyLookie, fallen from the ranks of the guides: you're a good boy, whatever your name is,' she said, bending down to pet him.

You took it in, the curve of her. She was wearing a white top that rode up a little. A top maybe a bit too nice for just a dog walk? If that's all it was. You were lingering too long. Someone, you knew who, had texted you twice in the last five minutes. You heard it in your pocket. So did she. But you didn't check it.

'We better push on,' you said, as all four of you came back around the corner to where you started. 'Those bins won't urinate on themselves.'

Another laugh. Hee hee hee. You let it go into you.

'Push on so,' she said, with a wink. A wink that said to you: whatever you think is beyond your reach, you just need to stretch a little more assertively. You may have misread it. It might just have been an involuntary response to something in her eye. But you know it wasn't. And neither was your one in return. Even though you've been dulled against blunt stones for years you can still pick out a moment. In this one there was nothing but you and her and these animals and all your desires mixing in the air. Morality is just a little poem. Chemistry is an immutable equation. When you're presented with energy that has to be converted, you can't do anything except play your part in the transfer. Your dog was pulling you away from her then. Same way he's pulling you forward now.

'Did you get my text?' Susan asked when you got in that second time.

'No, sorry, phone must have been on silent. What did, you …?'

'We've no milk.'

'I can go back out? Give him another stretch.'

'We'll survive.'

★

You let her in again later. When you were rubbing Susan's feet on the couch and not really putting in much of a performance. Your hands were there but your head was elsewhere. You wouldn't describe her as classically beautiful. In fact, on paper, lots not great. But still her face kept swimming up. You could see beyond her over-prominent incisors. You could live with the indentation on her right cheek. You have far worse imperfections. Let's not judge each other too harshly or nobody would choose anyone. And that laugh. In a different register. Susan doesn't laugh at what you say. That's not her fault. She's heard it all before. It's not your fault either though. No, she's not beautiful. No more or less than Susan. Just different. Different, though, can be enough. Somewhere else to look. Looking isn't a capital offence, is it? And she had looked at you first. She got entangled in the leashes earlier and nearly twisted her ankle. You put a hand to her shoulder to stop her going over. And you left it there. You could feel the strap of her bra under your fingers. She could feel your hand resting there, same hand that was later rubbing your wife's foot, and she let it linger. You were simply making sure she was alright. Who would not do that? Are we to be animals to each other?

'You're not here,' Susan said.

'I am, I mean look at me? Hello, giving my classic foot rub?'

'You know what I mean.'

From then to tonight was just a slip and a slide. You let a routine establish. Same time every evening (minus weekends, too complicated). This took some discipline and resistance on your part. Obstacles emerged. Last Thursday, Ella was going to a sleepover and you had to walk her down to the house, on your route. You held on to your dog as you walked down the road talking to her.

'I don't really want to go on this sleepover,' she said. 'I am only going because she asked me.'

'Well that's a nice reason to do something.'

'Not really. Not if I don't want to.'

You thought about the men she'd decimate in the future. You pictured yourself consoling her future dumped boyfriends.

Coming towards you were your usual travelling companions. You couldn't cross the road for no reason. Way too obvious, and Ella would ask questions. But you couldn't have this either. Your dog pulled towards them, you pulled him back. The collision was unavoidable. Ella bent and started petting Luna. You kept your head down.

'Look at this lovely dog,' Ella said.

'Yes, she – it's – a lovely dog,' you said.

'What's your name, doggie?' Ella said.

'Luna,' her owner, the absolute stranger, said.

'Our dog is called Lookie,' Ella said.

'Is he really?' she said. Don't mess now, you thought. You know not to mess, don't you?

'Well, come on Ella. We need to get going.'

'Luna is more like the dog we should have,' she said as you crossed the road.

By not even looking at Luna's owner, you bound yourselves closer. You caught up with her at the usual spot after.

You've been faithful. To your routines and to your companions on it, as the compass of your walks gradually extended. Through parks and by riverbanks, you have shared details that shouldn't leave a house. How Ella talks to you. How far away she feels. What Susan likes. What she doesn't. And she reciprocated. There'd been a long-term thing but it ended. No kids, no mess, and no one currently. That was all made clear.

'So why did you break up, if I can …?' you asked, as you came back to what was now the corner where your walks end.

'Because he just wasn't really there. He was in the room but just, not, you know?'

'I do,' you said, unsure if you were speaking of yourself or your wife, remember her, or both of you.

'But sometimes, you just want someone to share things with. You know what I mean? Like a funny thing happened at work, and who do you tell? The fridge? Now I find I'm telling you. Is that weird?'

'No, not at all. I'm glad you tell me. I'm happy to be the someone.'

'I am too,' she said, and smiled, and waited.

'And, um Lookie here is too. As long as you don't reveal his true identity.'

Again, three notes, that laugh. Enough for tonight.

You already have someone, you thought, lurching home. You're supposed to be the someone to that someone. But now for no good reason you seem to have another one. Christ, you know her brothers' names and occupations. You're sketchy enough on some of this with Susan.

You could see why people have religion in their lives. Coming back relentlessly to the same spot in service of a wild idea that might come good. And on that walk home last night, the imprint of her laugh still on you, you made an oath. You resolved that if there was an opportunity to convert idea into action you would take it. Just to show you are not dead. *Can you hear me down here? In this dark four-chambered cavern. I've been buried alive. If you can hear me get help. Or come down here for a while, if you're free. Bring your dog if you want.* So on towards your destination you go. To where you're meant to be by now.

You had your final warning as you left tonight.

'I forgot to tell you,' Susan said, as you put on your coat. 'Weirdest thing. I was walking Lookie this morning, and this woman was jogging, coming towards us.'

'Uh-huh.' You kept your head down, untangling the leash and clipping it on his collar.

'And Lookie pulled me so hard towards her that I dropped his leash. I thought my shoulder was going to pop. He jumped up on her and started licking her. He never does that. So embarrassing.'

'That's weird,' you said, to the dog's ear.

'Isn't it? And she seemed fine with it.'

'Maybe she just liked dogs.'

'The weird thing was, I thought I heard her say hello Lookie.'

You pulled at his collar and stayed down with him.

'It's on his tag. She must have read it, I guess?'

'Yeah. That's the only possible explanation. Isn't it.'

You stood up, too quickly, and felt the blood rush. You faced towards the door and felt eyes on you. You could have surrendered. *Susan. I've become sort of, well, whatever I've become, I'm sorry about what happened. Nothing has happened by the way but I'm still sorry. Let's open a bottle of wine on a Tuesday. Let's have one of those date nights that are all the rage. Let's forget and remember what was before all of this. Let's not blame each other.* But you had somewhere to be.

'He's got to get out or he'll go mad,' you said, and pulled the door behind you, and let him pull you forward. That's just his nature. Men and male dogs are more alike than men and women, as you recently said to another woman. A not-her woman.

Is she willing you? Is Susan saying go ahead, step on the landmine? Is that what she wants? Does she not even care? Does that make it better or worse?

You're now where you're meant to be. But she is not. You and your dog walk the road alone. You walk to the corner, down to her door. You know where she lives. You've stopped outside with her enough times, prolonging, looking, loitering with intent. Maybe her run-in this morning was the end of it. Maybe she's wised up. Someone has to.

You look up. She's at the window. She's gesturing to the door. She is taking the step you wouldn't. You're in a dumbshow. You're invited to play the part of gentleman caller.

What is your will? What will you?

Will you go towards the door? Will you find it open? Will you cross the threshold, your dog in tow? Will she descend the stairs? Will she take your hand and say *what kept you*? Will you enter a room with her, closing the door onto a privacy afforded at last? Will you hesitate, hear yourself say stop, stop and go back to the idea before the thing itself, you need that more than this? But your chemistry will be altered and the thought will not take. You will, if you will it, convert the energy of desire into the fire of action. The action will burn fast and be gone in a white moment. And in the exchange other compounds will be created but they won't have names yet. These new elements will fill your lungs and burn slowly, poisoning you from within over a half-life. But all of that will lie ahead of you. In this moment there will be only heat.

Or will you not? Will you instead look away and shake your head, and so will she, and that will be that? You'll move on up the road. You'll let Lookie guide you in the correct direction. You'll envision the avoided afterness. Lying there, your head hot in her hands. Saying what? Committing to what? Soft whispers will start the new phase. Then the chat will come. *I forget to tell you what happened at work today.* The chat that is as dull as it is different. From there to *you forgot to take out the bins* and sour glances is a hop and a skip. You'll walk past your daughter on the way to school a year from now with her mother and they'll look through you. You'll let the new fire go out and discover that a one-bed flat in Dundrum is the bitter dividend of desire.

You'll turn away, won't you? You'll lash up the road and turn for home. She doesn't know where you live. You've never walked that way. When you're safe, you'll say to Lookie, we had a close one there, didn't we? We should be more careful. We should find a new route. Good boy. You're a good boy. It's alright to look around. But you have to stay tight. You'll stand at the end of your driveway and look at your house. You'll see Ella doing ballet on the living room couch and Susan changing the bed sheets upstairs. You'll estimate the energy it would take to destroy two lives. And the energy it would take to create a new one. Your difference engine will give you the answer: Not worth. You, her, them, it. You will have a little word with yourself. You will fall in love again with someone soon, you always do. But this time, if it kills you, it will be your wife.

You stand here, at the gate. You're being pulled now by your dog. You're pulling back and holding your ground. The leash won't snap. But something's got to give.

ISHO 27

BARRY: To think, when we first met, you were just the old man at the window. 27A.

Aidan: I like the window. I paid four good euros for the privilege.

B: Not sure you got your money's worth.

A: And you were stuck in the middle. 27B.

B: Yeah. You didn't really respect the shared armrest rule.

A: There's a rule?

B: It might just be my rule.

A: And young Cian was in the aisle.

B: He didn't respect the rule either.

A: We did it to annoy you. The window and the aisle pressing in on the middle.

B: Conspiring strangers. I should have known from the start.

A: So there's your beginning, I suppose. Three strangers settling into their row on the red-eye.

B: Yes. That's where I'm starting. And you'll take a look at it? If I can get it down?

A: Of course. Let me know how you go. Now get your head down and get on.

★★

27B: We have one rule. One immutable rule on the FR118 Dublin to Gatwick Dep 0740 Arr 0910 – apart from all the other rules that Camilla, who's in charge of the cabin today, is going to take us through when we are doors-armed and cross-checked. It's this: *you don't talk.* You'd want to be stone-cold mental to fire up the chat in here. We'll open one eye and glare until you're shushed back into your fully upright position. This isn't the banter bus. This is the coffin ship. We are not all going on our summer holiday. We are on our way to work. I'm back Weds night. Could be worse. Could be Fri. Could be a whole lot better. Could be at the end of all this. To get to the end you have to go through the middle. And in life, like Ryanair seating algorithms, you mostly get middle. Four euros for window or the aisle. Or take your chances. I'll gamble. 27B it is. Neither here nor there. Look down the row at my travelling companions this morning. A and C, you're not regulars. Ten months into this you get to know faces. Window is old man and what do we call your kind in the aisle seat these days? Youth? Millennial? Doesn't matter. What matters is sleep. Let me climb into my 55-minute bed in the middle.

27C: On plane now. See you in a while!! New beats to bring you. Fun times ahead.
May need a disco nap first #redeye #sleepycian
[Photo of can of Red Bull] Has to be done! #givesyouwings
This has to be done.

27B: Aisle-boy, the convention is you stand up or compress yourself so I can get in? Or is this your first time on a plane? Head in phone, headphones on. Do you mind coming out of your sensory deprivation tank for a minute? You're in my way. Tap on the shoulder. Turn your bearded jaw up to me. How very punchable it is. IT consultant on track for Senior Partner slaps down snow-flake in pre-flight seat bust up. Everyone over forty sides with him. Keep it together. Get past this man-child.

27C: You in here, man?
27B: Yeah. If I could just ...
27C: No bother, buddy.

27B: *Man.* Yes I suppose if you're what twenty-two and I'm forty-seven then I am a man, compared to you. But we don't need age to make that distinction. Look at you. You're wearing three-quarter-length pastel pants at 7 a.m. on a Monday, and Princess Leia Headphones like you're going to drop a DJ set mid-flight. Look around you, sonno. Everyone here is in a suit and going to work. Where are you going? Tell you where you're not going. Senior Partner. You're not on track to senior anything. So sorry that you have to take all your worldly possessions off my seat. I could wait and see if an aisle or window opens up but as Camilla has said *we are operating a full flight today* and *if passengers could step in from the aisles as soon as possible* and you are not helping the situation. You're making me look like the problem. When the problem is you. Glacially gathering your magazines and your chargers and your oh my god *second identical set of headphones.* Why would you? One was too many, *buddy.*

27C: [Search] Cool bars open early Camden
Fun things to do in Camden
Best shops Camden
What will I do in Camden. What am I going to do.
Jesus man if you huff or puff any louder you'll blow the wings off. Fucsake. Just sit down will you.

27B: Did you get all your little toys? I'm not going to get a USB stick up the ass? Fall into the malignant middle. Look to my right. Window guy, guessing seventyish. Bit long in the molars for this? I know seventy is not supposed to be old anymore. But come on. From where I'm sitting it's end of days. No disrespect. It's not your fault. But you're closest to the clouds. Next one out. No way you're going over for work. No, you seem more on a visit to the brother or something. Herringbone blazer, argyle jumper, shit-brown cords. International old-man uniform. I could lose my mind and all I hold dear but I will never – mark me – *ever* – wear cords. I'm wearing a Reiss Ivy Check Stone slim fit and River Island Royal Blue non-iron shirt. Get two smart days out of it. Wear a proper suit, you are in armour invincible. Mister Millennium here is under the impression it's OK to wear shoes without socks and pants that would make Tintin wonder. Does he really believe his ankles are worthy of attention? Or is he planning a spot of whelk-shelling on the Thames before his early cool bars in Camden? Oh I can see your grand plans for the day, bud. Your phone is the size of a small television. You have 18 notifications. Nice to be wanted. I have some too.

Barry, You've unlocked our secret deal! Expires Midnight!
Congratulate Peter Ridley for 8 years at G7 Solutions
Agadir is calling your name, Barry. Book now and save 25%

I have not unlocked anything. I may also expire before midnight. Peter, my commiserations. Agadir though. Did Google it last night. The way these fucks follow your every whim and fling it back at you. Agadir. Sultry Moorish air. Dark reds and yellows in the souks and Atlas Mountains in the distance. Possibly. Possibly calling my name across the desert. Have to cross this sea first. Go towards the citadel and bring riches home. Camilla, once you've done your final checks, send us off with a battle cry, will you? Advance, you suited crusaders. Be ye warned, as you wake in Woking, Wiltshire and Wherever-the-Fuck on Thames, from your village-fêted tally ho howzat weekend. Merry Round the Maypole you go, Toby, Tristian and Tallulah, but look to the sky: we're on our way across the sea to pillage in pinstripe. But give us 55 minutes. First we need to sleep.

27A: I hope she is happy to see me. I hope we can be happy to see each other again. *It would be nice to see you again Aidan after all this time, but I am not in a fit state to travel.* I am. I will come to you. I wrote that I would. I will travel from Crumlin to Tooting. Wonder how many people have made that journey. Doubt anyone else onboard is going that way today. We all come from different places to sit together for a short while here and then head off in our own directions on the other side. Separate, briefly together, separate again. I know where I am going. A plane and a train and a bus and a short walk. I printed it off. I have time to gather my thoughts. I've had a good while to do that. A long trek and a short walk, over eighteen years and a few more hours.

27B: Two years max, they said. Step up. Cover London. You'll need to be there more. Three days a week OK? Not forever of course. Two years max. And then. 'Then' meaning Senior Partner. Two years is nothing. Run it down. 54 more Mondays like this, give or take. That is countdownable. Notch it off. Another morning in the dark. Let this be a middle that leads to a gilded finale. Senior Partner. Profit share.

27A: This lad next to me is up to a queer thing. Blowing air into one of those neck cushions. Like a little life jacket. Why would you not just buy one of those squidgy ones? They're two for 20 euros. He is wearing cologne. Too much. Too fresh. Took a complimentary blast of it going through the duty free, I'd say. Always been attuned to smells. Strange what's supposed to make us more intoxicating. Sandalwood and birch. Why not smell like you smell? Be yourself. That's a lot to ask though. I didn't put on anything today. Could have made more of an effort maybe. The jacket is new. Is it a bit too new. Not sure how new jacket *and* cologne would land with Alice. Get a load of you, back from the dead and stinking up Tooting Broadway, fragrant as you like. Wonder has her accent gone English. Easy to slip into it, I'd say. You can change to fit in or you can be as you are. Which is harder? This buck in 27B has black lines under grey eyes. Not much in his lungs. Put your back into it son. If that's all the breath you have God help you.

27C: Craic zero to negative here. Old work people zzz
Let me know when ur awake x
Delete x
Heart emoji
Delete. Calm down will you.
Smile heart plane. *Hide in the middle.*
Smile plane wave.
Smile and wave. Royal mess I'm getting into here. Will you see me coming a Camden mile off? Come over Cian, she said. Be great to see you. What Cian? You what? Ah sorry man. Didn't mean like that. She said, come over be great.

Just something you say though. You don't say don't come over it'd be fucking weird. Which is it. Where are we? We'll see when I see you.
See you when I see you!
Leave it. She wakes up to ten messages? Jesus man. Beats per minute. Slow it down.

27B: Have this down to a fine art, if anything about this was remotely artful. I travel light. Inflatable cushion means less bulk in the bag, less strain on the neck. Blow it up again. It's held a year of my weakest Monday breath. My backpack fits under the seat in front of me like it's supposed to. Laptop charger travel-size toothbrush socks jocks paracetamol deodorant. Gandhi, I think it was? Died owning his glasses and a rice bowl? My baggage is positively excessive in comparison but something elemental about it. Nothing I do not absolutely need in the next seventy hours. Good way to go through life. I glide through security. It's a hard right to the priority queue. They will let you through if you look like you know what you're doing. I do. Tiny gains. Five minutes shaved off the wait every Monday. Over a year that's two hours more in bed. If I offered you two hours in bed right now would you take it? My point exactly. Read about some project where they're trying to engineer mice to not have to sleep. Wrong way, science. We don't need more hours awake. That leads to just more time wasted. That's all this is. Travel is counterfeit purpose. As is my destination. Sit in a conference room. Strategy, actions, bullet-pointed nothings. Nobody's going to say, you know what Barry? That meeting in London today, that was your life's glittering moment. It's a step towards it though. Senior Partner. Tenured and untouchable.

27A: That's a handy contraption.

27B: No Christ no. Don't start. Rules? Also I am mid-inflation and if I answer it's air out to you that could be in here and I am trying to be efficient, no wasted effort. But. But. Let's not be bastardos of the runway. Gatwick East Croydon London Bridge Liverpool Street, save your fight for the other side. Don't be like that to one of your own.

27B: It is, yeah. Takes up less room.
27A: You're well set anyway. I'd say you've done this once or twice.
27B: Every Monday.
27A: Hard old station.
27B: Ah. Well used to it.
27A: You can get used to anything. As the fella says.

27B: If I put on my eye mask he will get the signal. This is not going to be a chitter-chatter. I am not surrendering vital sleep to you. I don't care if I look like an amateur ninja. Even a pressurised jolting doze is a bulwark against the nine-meeting day ahead. Close my eyes and enact the I'm-done-talking protocol.

27A: Every Monday. I'd say that's taking a toll. You can get used to anything. But that is not a reason to. You can slip into habits and get stuck in them for years. You can visit a woman in a town. You can slip into a situation with her. You can watch her make a choice to move away to London and away from you because you won't make the move. You can try and slip back into life with your wife and kids. You can try and let the woman slip out of your mind. But your mind has got used to turning to her and back in she slips when you're lying there. You can stay by your wife's side as she slips away and you can still slip into the other thought, your mind has no sense of decency. You can slip back into the perfume your daughter has taken to wearing. You can ask her what it is. You can go into a shop and spray some of it on a card and take it home and put it by your bed. You can wait. You can let years slip through you. You can hear from someone that she's alone, same as you. You can wonder. You can write a letter and stand over the postbox with it in your hand and wonder what you're at, before dropping it in and hearing your heart thump with it. You can get an answer. You can go. You can go and see an old acquaintance who is on her own now too in London. You can choose to do this. You don't have to explain yourself. It's nobody's business. I'll chance my day has more hope than yours, my inflatable friend. Go on to sleep if you want. I'm awake. I can look out the window and wait.

27B: Cushion inflated, eye mask on. Armour in place. Sleep isn't coming though. Some day I will burn these possessions. A little bonfire of the commuters. Not yet though. Coming up on halfway. Most of the time it is just the middle until you look back and you can say oh that was the start of the end. You can't see it from where you're sitting. Three of us in a row here. Arranged like the three ages of man and I'm in the middle. You start out young with a question. Takes a while for it to form. Halfway in, settle on an answer. At the end maybe you say, that wasn't the answer, or the question. But it's too late to back up. Taxiing down the runway. See the shape of things to come. Contort yourself, push down into the mould. Senior Partner. Assigned parking space. Drive into the space that's been allocated.

27C: Want to talk to you about something later. Nothing big. Just something. Don't worry x
It's just an x. not xx. Ex Ex. Could mean absolutely removed. Or back together again.
Send a picture?
What do you look like? Reverse camera. Don't send her a picture of the safety instructions.
Look like a tool. Fucking hair why won't you obey me. Delete. Thumbs up. Look dorky on purpose? Looks dumb as shit. Delete. Hold up the headphones.
Present for you!
Don't send. Just get there and then. Present for her. Delete.

Camilla: Dublin London Dublin London Dublin London Dublin. These ones are sleepers. Not drinkers. Easy. But may not buy enough. May not sell enough. May not make target for sales. Push scratch cards. Someone maybe feels lucky. Selling cigarettes whiskey perfume at this time does not work I keep telling them. These are things for the other end of the day. Safety demonstration. Nobody is listening. I am not listening and I am the one doing it.

27A: She's good now at what she does, this one. Pay her heed. Some of them I'd say, just going through the motions. But she has a way about it. It says *I'm doing this for you. I might just save your life.* She has a job to do and she's going about it the right way. I have a job ahead too, and I'm going about it. The right way, who can say? The only way I have left.

> **Camilla:** If the oxygen masks fall, attend to your own first before helping others. Do not worry if you don't feel anything. Oxygen is flowing.

27A: Cruel but necessary steps for survival. I cannot help you if I'm slowly choking. I have to save myself before I can turn to you. Wife, child or otherwise. You would do the same to me and I wouldn't blame you. It's what I did and will do again.

27B: I have one eye out of my mask. I'm paying attention, Camilla. Close attention. Let my eye rest on something unharsh before it closes. Tell me more, you dark-eyed philosopher of the skies.

> **Camilla:** In the highly unlikely event of a landing at sea, lights will guide your way.

27B: See those lights guiding the way. Japanese lanterns stringing back to Sandymount. Follow them and rise unscathed on the shore. It's a nice image, Camilla. But in that unlikely event there is going to be no gentle landing at sea and no bright lights to guide. This is not a hot-air balloon where we'll softly crest onto a wave and doff our top hats to the dolphins, awaiting a passing tug boat to haul us aboard. Thank you for inviting us to review the safety instructions, but it will not play out in the laminated way. Let's level here, Camilla. It's highly unlikely, but surely more likely with every roll of the dice. Tiny shift but the needle moves. Fly twice a week for two years. That change in the odds must register. On a microscopic level, risking my life for this reward. Senior Partner. Air miles. And if it happens, this unlikely but increasingly possible event, we will slot at an unnatural angle into the dark waves, some screaming, some heads down and, if we are lucky, most lulled into unconsciousness from the pressure drop on descent. We will have one last dream and wake no more. *They died instantly.* There is no instantly though. We move through time and live through each instant including and especially the last. We will have time to comprehend that the end is rising up from the earth to meet us and in that moment we will know ourselves and the light unlit within. If it comes to it Camilla, will you get me out of here alive? I would do it for you. *His last act was one of remarkable bravery.* Be remembered well.

Camilla: Bear in mind your nearest exit may be behind you.

27B: I'll bear it deeply. How many exits have I passed? Could have turned left towards California. Could have gone there with her, instead of listing the pros and cons aloud. She made the choice for you. It's where I want to be, she said. It's home. There's no point fighting that. We are on different paths, she said. All the exits you could have taken but ignored because you are on the S.P.-runway awaiting clearance. We can't turn back. The doors are locked and we are pushing forward. Maybe you'll guide the way Camilla. Maybe we will attend to each other. Let's not rule out even the most unlikely events. Did you look on me and think, of all of them, I am *especially* concerned about your comfort and safety? Two people circling the earth reach out to stop each other from spinning out of orbit. Could happen. I was on a path but I got diverted. You could be my exit, right in front of me. I could get to know your family. A small farmhold outside Riga maybe. I could tend to sheep and dress quite differently. In the evenings we will over and over tell each other the tale of our chance meeting. How we changed directions. I'll look at you and think on how something highly unlikely could come to pass.

Camilla: Why is this one looking at me? Sad small eyes. Fat small face. Like a turkey. Turkey in a bad suit. Grabber maybe. Grabber sleeper panicker puker what are you. 27C is nicer looking. Not good shoes though. At least looks like going some-where fun. When I say headphones off I will touch him on the shoulder. 27B, put your mask on and cover your sad eyes. You are not a problem when you sleep. You are just a closed face. This weekend home to my family. See my father and mother. See maybe Tomasz. It's only Monday though. Do this forty times before then. I will see some of you again before the weekend. Over and back. You are migrant workers. You should stay in one place, there or here. This is not a good life.

27A: We are taxiing down the runway. Why that word. Not like we're going to pick up anyone on the way. Would be handy if that was how planes worked. Stick an arm out and whistle and they stop for you. Where are you headed mate. Graveney Road Tooting Broadway or as close as you can drop me thanks. I will walk along that road each step short-ening the years of distance between us. Finally going. But not gone yet.

27C: Not gone yet. Sitting here ages. Sending you a mix I made just now. Hope you like it.
[Sending: runway.mp3]
Not gone yet but will be soon. I am going to be there with you. I'm going to ask you. Should have asked you before. Want to stay here? Want me to come with you? I'm visiting some friends in Camden and if you're around be great to meet up, that's what I told you. I'm not visiting friends. I'm coming for one reason. We should both stay in one place. Here or there. Wherever you want. In the morning when I wake up you're the first thing. If I don't tell you this my head will burst. Tell me to leave or let me stay but either way, today, I'm asking. I can take the answer. I can't take not asking.

27B: Not gone yet. Here we go. Force pinning me back. Mask off again. The noise of the music leaking from his headphones ruining hope of sleep. Not supposed to have those on. Can interfere with the instruments. Don't you listen when people say what to do? Camilla has tapped you on the shoulder. Do you know how lucky you are? Do you know how much is ahead of you? You're not even a quarter down the runway. Are you going to waste it?

27C: Old guy at the window just blessed himself! In the name of the seat belt and the sick bag and the holy wing-span amen. Have to switch this off cu soon!

27A: Dear God let today work. Let me be not making a fool of myself. Or if I am let me not be the only one. Let there be two of us in it.

>   27C: What's happening?
>   27B: I don't know. What's happening?
>   27C: Why are we turning?
>   27A: I think we are in trouble.

Camilla: We're banking. This is too sharp. Look at Marta. She is looking at me, eyes are saying why, I don't know why. No call from cockpit. Tell us what is happening. Red light flashing now. Marta is talking to the Captain. She's saying to me to say to them.

>   **Camilla:** Ladies and gentlemen we are having some
>   difficulty please keep your seat belts fastened please stay
>   calm and in your seats

>   27B: Jesus. Jesus.
>   27A: Give me your hand.

Camilla: Tomasz has blue eyes. He looks at me and says hey, Camilla. Why don't you come back here? Why don't you stay here with me? You should be here. He says this with his eyes, they look into mine and say, what do you want? He is an unsafe person though. Drives too fast. You will get yourself killed some day, I said to him when we were driving into the countryside in the night. You got to go sometime, he said, lighting a cigarette and laughing. I won't crash. You are safe with me, he said. I looked at one of his eyes from the passenger seat. You look at someone and you see what you want. The part of them that you want is all you see. I see wild eyes and smile and danger excitement and he sees same in me I think and this is what we want to see in each other. Say it to me, Tomasz. Say stay. Not just with your eyes say it and make it real. Some day he would have said it and I would say. I would have said. Before this. This. Trained for this. This is it. Say what nobody ever wanted to hear—

Camilla: Brace. Brace. Brace.

★★

A: So, I read it.
B: And? Don't leave me hanging.
A: That's kind of what you're doing, Barry.
B: I know it's not finished.
A: Well, you know how it ended.
B: I don't really want to go into that.
A: Think you're past turning back. As the fella says.
B: I'll get it down.
A: Few more things ...
B: Here we go.
A: Do you want feedback or not?
B: Sorry. Go on.

A: It's your story and all that, and great that you're back at it again, but you're making yourself out to be a bit of a bastard.

B: If anything I'm underplaying it.

A: And I wasn't quite so, desperate.

B: I'm underplaying that too, based on what you've told me.

A: And poor Cian is just texts and headphones. He's a lot more than that.

B: I can't get it all in, Aidan.

A: You have to get us down. Start there and work back. Meet in the middle, as you might say yourself.

B: Let me give it a go. Would you take another look?

A: What else would I be doing?

★★

Excerpt from Incident Report on FR118

At 08:07:22 on Feb 6 2017 during take-off on Runway 1 Flight FR118 suffered a complete loss of power in Engines 1 and 2. Per Standard Operating Procedure Captain Doyle assessed the stop/go decision. The aircraft was in excess of V1 decision speed and hence a Rejected Take-Off was not possible. Captain Doyle rolled west off Runway 1 and completed rotation to re-approach. Runway 1 approach angle was deemed unfit for safe landing. Runway 2 was cleared for approach. The aircraft burned out two tyres and suffered minor damage to undercarriage but stopped successfully 170 feet short of Runway 2 end. Fire and emergency services were dispatched. A full evacuation was undertaken and managed effectively by crew. No injuries were sustained. Some passengers were treated for shock and all were offered counselling, and several have taken up this offer. One opted to rebook on the next departing flight, despite advice to the contrary. We understand that some passengers have kept in contact over the months since the incident and have developed friendships post-counselling. The Captain and crew are to be commended for their calm and assured handling of the situation, avoiding a potentially far more severe outcome. The incident is now closed and the aircraft has returned to service.

★★

A: Really?

B: Well, that's what happened. Like, officially.

A: *Officially.* I seem to remember a bit before that, though.

B: It's the bit I can't really handle.

A: That's what you went to counselling for. You've already talked about it, right? Or did you skip over that in your sessions and focus on the stress of having no parking space.

B: I've talked it out so much.

A: So put it down. What you were really thinking about? When we were, what did they call it? Wasn't falling ...

B: Rolling. I don't really know.

A: Don't try and fool an old man, now. You've plenty to say about going up in the world. What have you to say about coming down.

B: I ... here's what it is. When you think, this is it, I am going to die, you expect, I don't know.

A: A moment of clarity.

B: Yeah. Like your body will suffuse with some protective endorphins and fear will leave your nerve endings and there will be some light. *Brace, brace* Camilla was saying. *Embrace, embrace* is what they should say.

A: Everybody grab somebody and hold on for dear life.

B: Well, yeah. And you'll think about everything in an instant, your whole life. And it'll all just, resolve.

A: You don't though. We know that now. You've time for one thing. Don't you.

B: I was, this is – I remembered being at home, in my room, when I was twelve. I had a little red notebook. I was writing down words that I liked the sound of. I don't know why. My Aunt had been over and she was talking about someone, some singer, as having the light within, I don't remember who. But those words. A crack in the wall opened. I wrote it down. I've lost the notebook but I could, in that rolling moment, see it written so clearly. *The Light Within.* I wrote a story about someone who could swallow light and it was in the school magazine. And that was the end of my glittering career in literature.

A: No it wasn't.

B: No, really it was. All out of my system now.

A: Don't do that to yourself.

B: Do what.

A: Draw a line under yourself. You used to write. Then you stopped and did something else. And now you are doing it again. It's not out of your system. It is your system.

B: So what was your this-is-it thought?

A: Changing the subject. Is that what you do in your important meetings?

B: I'm trying to bring you and Cian more into it. Per your feedback.

A: I thought, I won't see Alice today. After all this waiting. And I think if your last thought is of a certain woman, that's not a bad way to bow out.

B: And you did see her. You got on the next plane, I still don't know how.

A: It added a certain frisson to our reunion, I'll say that. I conquered death to get to Tooting Broadway.

B: You old charmer.

A: Oh, that's more Cian's territory.

B: I think about what I made of him. Before we took off, I was looking at him thinking, what are you all about? With your headphones and your gear. You're a child.

A: There's a bang of jealousy. Maybe you wanted his youth. Or, God forbid, his shoes.

B: What can I say? Senior Partner prick in the making.

A: It only took an emergency landing to knock that out of you.

B: As we were rolling, I looked over at him. I was thinking, I should be minding you. I should put my arm around you. You're too young to go. I was thinking about you too, Aidan. At least you and me had a decent run at it.

A: Decent might be pushing it.

B: I was useless, in that moment, wasn't I?

A: You can't ask too much of yourself.

B: You really should, though.

A: Talked to Cian lately?

B: We text. He sends me his mixes. I'm listening to one now.

A: I was wondering what that racket was. I must get up to one of his concerts.

B: You should. They're called sets though. It's not the philharmonic, old man. You might want to bring protective headphones.

A: I'd say he'd sort me out with a pair or two.

B: Bring Alice. She'd like it.

A: You should come over. We'll all go out.

B: Yeah, I'm not, you know ...

A: Not flying?

B: No. I don't know how you just –

A: I had to get here. What are the odds of it happening twice?

B: You and Cian. Pair of you on your way. To see about a girl. I should've swapped seats and let the two of you natter on.

A: You had your – interesting thoughts about Camilla. Maybe you should get in touch? I'm sure the airline could pass on your, what would Cian say? Deets?

B: I've no idea about her. I made all that up. I only know what you guys have told me about yourselves. I'm only writing it down because you asked me to.

A: I thought it'd help. Something to do while you get back on track. Senior Partner or otherwise.

B: I'm going to quit today, by the way. I've decided. They said I could change roles. Base myself here for a while. But you know. Fuck it.

A: Good man. Attend to your own mask. *Parking space.* Is that what you were hanging in for?

B: They're quite the perk.

A: Listen. I have a word for your red book, before I go. *Isho.*

B: What's that.

A: Japanese. Means last wishes or will. I've been reading about plane crashes.

B: That sounds healthy.

A: Japan Airlines 123. They had twelve minutes in descent. They weren't as lucky as us. Crashed in the mountains, this was years ago. Some of the passengers wrote their *isho*, on the way down. *Help your mother. Be good to each other and work hard. Look after our children. Please live bravely. I love you. I am sorry.* There's a book of them.

B: I'd like to read them.

A: I'd like you to write them. Ours. What was really in our minds in that moment. I've told you mine. Cian did too. Get them down. And your own.

B: Our last wishes.

A: Not our last. We can still act on ours. Unlike those poor souls in Japan. Isn't that what we should be doing? There. That's your end. Go and finish it. I'll give you another chance.

B: I'll try.

A: And look up the translation of *Issho*, too, while you're at it. With two 's's. It has a few meanings that might help you.

B: *Isho. Issho.*

A: Bless you.

B: Aidan, you're some bollix.

★★

Isho 27A: I am sorry Alice. I am sorry I didn't make it to see you. I wanted to say to you that you never left my heart. I waited so long to find you again but I left it too late. I am sorry to my wife who I will never see again, and my children, who will discover that I was going after a woman who was never to be talked about again. My last act was trying to find her before it was too late. I passed go/no go. I am not ashamed. There is no shame in surrendering to the heart.

Aidan: That's where I was. Now you've got me down. And you should know, my kids are happy for me and Alice. We're all too old for shame. I shouldn't have been so doubting. Barry, are we not the luckiest people alive? What will you do with your luck?

Isho 27C: Did it send. I love you. In London I was going to tell you. By the Camden Lock I was going to put these head-phones on you and play this to you and say: I love you and I want to be here with you. I was going to kiss you into the mix while we both listened to it. Did it send. Do you hear me. I love you. That's all I wanted to say.

Cian: It did send. We're good man. You know what she said. I don't read much stuff tbh but hey great that you're writing. It was a freaky day. All over quick though. You weren't that much of a dick really! All just got to you for a minute. Don't worry about putting more of me in. I was mainly thinking about the mix and getting over to see her and yeah I probably did have too much gear with me so fair enough. I took the boat and the train a few days later. Wi-Fi strong as an ox all the way. Come visit us in Camden sometime? There's a cool bar you'd like I think. Hey it's great you, me and Aidan have kept in touch isn't it? What are the odds? Did you like my mix btw?

Isho 27B: As I approached the end, what happened was this. This young man, in 27C. He heard me say it. He put his arm around me. We are going to make it man, he said to me. He was the one embracing me. This old man in 27A. He heard me say it too. He put his arm around me too. Be brave now, he said. And I let them. I let them leave their final thoughts and embrace me as I said, apparently, over and over:

27B: The Light Within. The Light Within. The Light Within.

I kept saying it. That's what Aidan told me, after. And I've no reason to doubt him.

Why did you keep saying that, he said, as we were being bussed back into the airport. I couldn't answer him then, I was still shaking. Not with the shock of what had happened to the plane. With the shock of what happened to me.

The light within. That's where I'd left myself. That's who I went back to save. The twelve-year-old who tried to swallow light, writing into my red book, asking a question. I put down childish things and went to work. I put on a grey suit and became someone else. All the time I was waiting beneath the waves. The red book reopened in the last instant.

Aidan asked me to give him my number, when they were checking us over. He got Cian's too. We should keep an eye on each other, he said, and winked at me. We had a moment up there. I'll give you a buzz sometime. Now if you bucks will excuse me, I need to get off to London, he said.

Isho: Testament, will, last wishes.
Issho: Together, in the same place, at the same time. What are the odds. Answer the question.
Issho: Lost book.

I know we need an ending, Aidan. But nothing ended that day. Something restarted. Sorry my dear old friend. You'll have to bear with me. I'd forgotten how endings work. I was stuck in the middle for a while. Now, finally, I'm on my way back to the beginning.

The light within is not yet out. Open again the red book. Write yourself back in.

Isho. Aidan. Cian. Issho. Camilla. California.
Oxygen is flowing.
Guide me on my journey.

SHINE/VARIANCE

OK, LATE, I KNOW WAS supposed to be home at 1 to pick
him up and do this thing and now gone 3 and just getting
out of office. In my defence: busy and, if honest, quite
challenging morning/afternoon so not fully ready to step
into festive season as parting words from James still
ringing re Quarter 4 full 14% off target and deep concerns. These justifiable as variance from target pronounced
and compounded by Quarter 3 variance and need to
address issues. Fully understand, I said, and committed
will get out there today and shake the tree. But have also
made counter-commitment at home. Texted Nicki:

> *Running late lots on any chance could push tree thing with*
> *Charlie to tomorrow?*
> *No. He's been waiting since 1.*
> *OK. On way. X*

Stop saying *on way* when nowhere near. This a problem
in Quarter 4 too. Have assured will come good but
nowhere near. Have texted Nicki again: *Outside now can*
you tell Charlie come out in 5 mins as have to do quick call in
car. Do not need to do call just do not want to go in.
Should make call. Should let James know working on
making Q4 good. But not actually doing. Already called
best prospects. All saying check in after Christmas let's

see in Jan enjoy the break etc. 'Enjoy' unlikely given 14% adrift and two days at best remaining before closeout.

Also, nice just sit in car take moment as house has full feeling. Full of kids. Kids fine. Generally fine. Just one thing would say and not critique of any specific individual but three is a lot no? House weather moves between extreme screaming and extreme tired. Piles of things everywhere. Piles of clothes in hall and on stairs. Piles of twins on floor eating crayons or similar. Nicki mainly asleep on couch when not actually correctly asleep in bed. Charlie often left to own devices as in literally just face lit by screen and seems content but that not active parenting. So nice if indulgent to stay in car and not step in just yet. Plus, enormous amount of together time ahead over Christmas. And possibly enormous more in Jan if Q4 undelivered as consequences clear in meeting. And feeling slightly woozy, coming down with something? Best not infect whole house. Possibly make Charlie sick too. Though promised today tree day, one-on-one special time, very important. Heard that in podcast on being a present parent which listened to on way home late last night.

Here he is. Why not smiling? Not looking forward to this? Very ungrateful if not as quite a sacrifice to do this today given challenges.

'Are you excited?' I ask.

'Why are you so late?'

'I was very busy at work, Charlie.'

'You're always busy.'

This unfair in my view but not wishing to start on sour note so leave it. Onto Sandyford road and head right, away from town. Nice to head towards mountains, away from things, as nature can have positive effect during challenging times many self-improvement experts say.

'So we're getting a tree?'

'Not a tree, Charlie. *The* Tree. The best most amazing tree.' Within our range which, as of this moment, is subject to pronounced downwards revision.

'Where are we going to get it?'

'I think we'll just scope out a few places? See what we like the look of?'

'Can I play on your phone?'

Give it to him. Watching fail videos. Kids falling off bed into pools etc. Unclear if people actually hurt requiring treatment, assume not as off-camera laughter. Switch on Xmas FM. Driving home for/Step into/ Thank God it's/All I want for. They are raising money for sick children: Give what you can at this Special Time. That is worst thing. What must it be like. Life devoted to care. At same time (horrible thought but) quite pure way to be? Parents of sick children, humble with noble statements: she's the light of our life and it has made us stronger more patient better people. When listen to them talking like this, as doing now on radio, feel slightly jealous. World excuses you for not having on-target Q4 and constantly tired if you have to deal with horrific illness or similar.

Our kids not sick. Not complaining or wishing otherwise of course. Our kids fine. Fine but not amazing. Look at other people's children, at carol service or school play, and see faces shining then look at own and thought is oh well. Can divide people into two groups: shining faces like lit from within and then non-shining dullish faces. Ours non-shining variety. Of course love but if can be objective for a moment would give them maybe

5 average on looks. Charlie maybe when was younger smaller smiling more would give solid 7 or in some light 7.5 but recently face not so cute as eleven now and sharper jaw where was puppy fat, gone from looking like adorable gerbil to more like fox. Twins have odd look about them. Twin mouths hanging open. Bad eyesight both and wearing glasses further disimproving look. May outperform over time as only three but currently drag down average score. This not their fault: Nicki/me not catwalk material, readily admit mid-table at best. Low score manageable when child but then grow up and world says, alright, nice that you're intelligent/caring etc. but we go mainly on looks here and you, well, you're OK but only OK. And confidence if not good, means you only get with other 5s or below within variance zone. If getting older, more desperate possibly, settle for a 4 or below. Distinct possibility grandchildren, if any, will be hovering around 3 or lower.

While deep worrying about how Charlie will end up with sub 5 wife and we get likely very basic-looking grandkids he interrupts.

'You have a text.'

'OK, I'll look at it later, I'm driving now,' as important to set example don't text and drive. Have seen the ads. Charlie obsessed with watching them. Children all smashed up funeral tears lone parent staring into middle distance if only hadn't been distracted by text.

'It's from James. *Need to speak urgently re Q4 variance. V concerned. Call pls.*'

This in Charlie's voice taking edge off? Or actually making worse?

'OK. Thanks.'

'Is James your boss?'

'Yes.'

'What's a Q4 variance?'

'It's when something isn't what you thought it would be.'

'Like a surprise?'

'Yeah, sort of. Do you like surprises?'

'It depends. Some surprises are like, oh wow a bike.'

'Yeah. That's on your list, I know.'

'But then you could also be told surprise! You have a serious illness.'

'Yeah.'

Serious illness? Must have picked up from radio just now. Lets things like this go into him. Like watched YouTube videos about deaf children hearing for first time, all tears emotional, and told teacher he used to be deaf and remembered first time hearing our voices. Crying in class with memory of. Had to clarify to teacher not case. Told him that making up things of this nature can be confusing for people. Just using my imagination, he said. Just to see what people would say. Don't want to crush imagination as this positive but need to watch, as imagination sometimes just lies.

'Do you need to call James? It's OK if you do,' Charlie is saying as we pull into tree place in Enniskerry. This now really pushing in on our special time and nothing I can do about Q4 in this moment.

'It's OK. I'll do it later. Let's get our tree first.'

We are in this, I guess would call, pleasant grotto. Realistically garden centre but effort with lights and canopy overhead goes some way to transform, bring small amount of magic/otherness. Can step into this moment? Leave Q4 in car? Get Charlie a hot chocolate from stand. They're also selling mulled wine in small plastic cups and yes why not no harm only tiny amount. Mulled wine hot and sweet and now catching in throat a bit overly cloying. Spill it onto a tree as ideally not drink-driving and destroying future lives on top of present challenges.

Man approaches and asks us what kind of tree we're looking for.

'We want the perfect tree,' Charlie says and smiles at me. At least listening in part to aspirational car talk. Definitely points for that.

Man takes one tree, shakes it out, shows to us. 'This is a 10-footer Norwegian non-shed.'

Looks very luxurious. 10 foot a lot of tree though.

'How much is it?' I ask.

'120.'

12 euros a foot. For something just in nature? Freely occurring? Actual moral right to charge for this?

'I think, just looking at it now, a bit big, no?'

'Depends on where you wanna put it, pal,' says man with tone counter-seasonal.

Ideas on where to put it arriving in mouth but do not share with man as has feel of moment that spills into faces pressing into each other and yeah? Oh yeah? type exchange and already enough going on.

'Would you have anything, maybe, a bit more ...'

'Modest?'

'Compact.'

Modest? In front of clearly son? Perhaps is actually moment for asserting with face? Show Charlie can't let world be all at you?

'I have 6 foot or 8 foot. Or, well I have 12 foot, but that's not ...'

'No, that's less ...'

'Compact. Yeah.'

He gets out a few more and props against wall. Charlie points to 6-foot one.

'This one looks OK.'

He's correct, does look OK. On small side. But actually more full, I think, in the branches than 10 foot. And not so dwarfing of people. Twins possibly terrified of large tree. If falls over causes injury then festivities ruined and trip to Emergency: *Oh that is a nasty gash, we do see this a lot, people should really get more compact trees.* Nicki shaking her head, *if only you had been more modest, this is what we get for overreaching.* Decorations have more impact if all bunched together in any case?

'So how much are we looking at for the 6 foot?' I say to man.

'80.'

'80?'

'Yep.'

This, just working it out, actually more expensive per foot than 10 foot? How does that work? Man just making up numbers now. Clearly some kind of spite tax applied.

Charlie touching its branches. Not seeing much in way of delight amazement in face.

'What do you think Charlie?'

'I think this one is fine.'

'Fine? Did we come all this way for fine?'

'I don't really mind what kind of tree we get.'

'Well you look around a bit. I just need to get something from the car.'

Before walking off lean in to Charlie.

'These are not good trees. We are under no obligation here.'

Wink at man. Does not wink back. Leave it. Point made.

Have cigarette behind car. Text James. *Will call shortly.* Not now. Charlie not really minding re tree, this disappoints. Needs to strive more. Charlie bit of a settler? If things just OK then he is happy. His Santa list a bit flat. Bike Football Goals. Ask for more? But also grateful he's not doing so. Picking up maybe this not great time to want for more? Happiness is reality minus expectations. This from mindfulness podcast. Sounds insightful and liked at time when breathing in through nose out through mouth as instructed but on reflection perhaps equation encouraging very low expectations. This is how end up with 5-ish life situation when ideally 8 plus target so quite large variance. Further problem with 'minus expectations' part being that expectations hard to control. Generally high and rising especially when looking around at other people while reality fixed or declining over time. Result equals happiness drifting downwards and possible long term to become negative. Maybe draw graph of this to illustrate point to Charlie as life lesson? Old enough would understand. Maybe become expert in happiness and striving for correct expectations and have podcast of own, write book on this? New direction? People change directions. Many gurus deeply unhappy then changed expectations and now extreme mindful and no longer striving/dealing with Q4 or similar issues.

Go back into grotto and find Charlie looking at another smallish tree.

'Let's get this one,' he says.

Choice looks bit dumpy in my view and limp in effect overall. Possibly am overthinking choice of tree. Tree not symbolic of reality vs expectations. Tree just tree. But still, not great tree and certainly not at proposed price per foot. Get out of here. Show man we are not settlers. Man not currently around though.

'What didn't you like about that tree?' Charlie asks when we are back in car and heading further up towards mountains.

'It was fine. We can always come back to that one. It's just, we might find a better one at the next place.'

Phone rings.

'It's James,' he says.

'Just leave it,' I say maybe too loudly, sharply, because in panic he pushes answer button and now James on speaker. Charlie holding phone up to me as will not let me drive and hold phone, family rule per the ads.

'James, hi, was just about to—'

'So where are we at, Martin?'

'I'm working on it. Was just talking to Nelson. Sounding positive.'

'Sounding positive as in closing today?'

'That's my read, yes.'

'So are you giving me a firm commitment?'

This a thing with him now. Firm Commitment. Tone gone very formal in last few weeks. Lots of follow-up emails. *We continue to be concerned. You have given me a Firm Commitment.* Expect then forwards to HR so all on record: *I told him this* and *he said that* and *he did not do that so we have no choice but to* etc.

'Yes. But I need more time to work it.'

'You have until close of play. As we discussed this morning. Do we need to go back over what we agreed?'

'No, we don't.' Can quite clearly recall what was agreed. Agreed not really the word though. He said what he wanted and said *can you make a Firm Commitment on this*. Didn't say 'or else'. But 'or else' clear.

'So close of play update?'

'Close of play.' As in two hours from now. He hangs up.

Charlie looks at me.

'Just work stuff,' I say.

Moving further up into mountains. Roads getting narrower and keep having to shift gears and tight uphill turns and not relaxing driving-home-for-xmas feeling more like rally conditions and light starting to fade.

See Charlie's jawline. He is clenching. Grinds his teeth at night. Anxiety maybe. What to be anxious about? Has no problems. Is looking out the window not talking not looking at phone. Car mood 4, 5 best.

'Don't want to watch your videos anymore?'

'No signal.'

This good. Out of range so not my fault. *Couldn't call you back apologies James was not able to get back to you by close of play can we pick up in Jan?* Q4 off. Accept this. Not going to make it. Calm peaceful feeling if just accept? Not feeling that right now. Feeling more sick, possibly altitude and wooziness combining with commitments turning more infirm by the minute.

'Who is Nelson?' Charlie asks. Remember he in car listening and not dumb.

'One of my customers.'

'Why did you say you'd just been talking to him?'

'Did I say that?'

'Yes.'

'Well, I was.'

I was. Just talked to him yesterday. He was clear no movement on order until Jan. But people say that and may just be looking for end of year discount to get it through. Waiting for me to make next move? Thinking I'm not pushing enough and someone more hungry would be pushing more? Someone else in his office right now shaking hands, going home to their family, Nelson deal done, get whatever tree they want? 3 for effort here. Now at entrance to Tibradden Woods.

'This is nice isn't it, Charlie? Two men in the mountains?'

'I'm a bit hungry,' he says.

'OK. We'll find something.' Also realise am hungry and this possibly contributing to current choices.

'There's nothing up here.'

'Let's get out and have a look around.'

Park and walk up path. Walking into woods, just me and Charlie, quite idyllic. Something to remember.

'It's getting a bit dark,' Charlie says.

'But kind of fun too?' I say.

'I guess.'

Humouring me? Unclear if genuinely terrified but press on. We snap through the dried pine on forest floor and come to a gap in the middle.

'What about this one?' I ask, and put hand on large tree. Easily 10 foot. More like 14. Serious tree.

'What do you mean?'

'I thought we could, like real men, you know, cut it down and bring it home.'

He's looking at me like are you real actual man in charge of things.

'You're not allowed to do that.'

'Who says?' Good chance to show you make own rules in life even if not always case.

'Isn't it stealing?'

'Stealing from who? It's nature, Charlie. Who owns nature?'

'How would we even get it down?'

'We could tie some ropes around it, and, I could get the car up this far, and ...'

'I saw an epic fail video where someone did that and the tree fell on their car and crushed it.'

That is, to be fair to him, possible outcome which would further compromise day. Also no ropes, just some twine in boot. Though annoyed at his limited and nega- tive thinking.

'Wouldn't it be fun just to get our tree, straight from nature, like this?'

'Dad, I think we should just go back and get the tree we were looking at in the other place. I don't like it up here.'

Look at him. Look at dark wood where we have ended up. What meant to be nice afternoon outing memory now stuff for future nightmares. And how would even get car up here, how sawing supposed to transpire. Not well formed as idea. None of today or Q4 thought out properly. Stop all of this. Urge to wander into woods on own and find quiet, peaceful, out of range place. Become hermit. Carve wood. Stay away from people. But have tasks responsibilities. Take Charlie's hand.

'Charlie. I'm sorry. You're right. This is not a good idea. I'm sorry I brought you up here. It was stupid. I'm just not feeling very well at the moment.'

'Are you going to die?'

'No.'

'My teacher said we are all going to die some day.'

'That's true. But not today.' This teacher idiotic. Not what you say to someone like Charlie, already death/ illness fully fixated.

'Are you in trouble at work?' Charlie asks as we go back down path to car.

'A bit.' Just let all out? If don't then just more lying, putting off and poor example. He now more aware than Nicki of how things stand. Stop hiding things. Account for where you're at. What is worst can happen? Everyone will know soon enough.

'But don't worry about it. OK? It's all going to be fine.'

Sit down on tree stump for a moment to catch breath and await idea to land. Moments like this when inspiration/epiphany comes for many gurus. Nothing coming except: get Charlie out of here.

'I don't mind what I get for Christmas,' he says, looking away from me at city lights vista below car park.

'OK. Well you've sent your list, so, just wait and see.'

'I know. But, if it's ... I don't mind if I don't get things.'

Charlie settling for less. Because of you drifting, off target. This is how you take the shine away from all of them.

Then have strong clear idea. As if can picture great outcome if just act on. Not epiphany, not that big. More of a piph. But still something. Like hand pushing towards obvious destination.

'Charlie. I'm going to get you something to eat. Then we are going to get a proper tree. First we just need to go somewhere.'

Pull into car park, very busy for a Friday afternoon. Lot of kids walking around. Then remember they are having the family Christmas party today. He told me when I suggested meet at his office on Fri to try and finalise things. *Can't do Fri family Christmas party at work let's meet in New Year have a good one.* But here I am in the area and was passing and thought well why not.

'Why are we here?' Charlie asking as we walk into reception.

'There's a man in here that I just need to have a quick chat with. It won't take long. And you will get free chocolate. Is that OK?'

'What man?'

'His name is David Nelson.'

'The Nelson you told James you were just talking to?'

'Yes.' Nelson who is idea that called from mountain. 'And I was talking to him, Charlie. I talked to him yesterday.'

'Yesterday is not just now.'

'It's close enough.'

Reception lady asks our names. We are not on family Christmas party list. Explain this probably because personal friend of David Nelson and he'd said to drop in and probably just didn't have time to update list. This sort of true as in previous years has said stop in if you want. Not this year specifically but surely standing invitation. Put arm around Charlie. Not going to put a boy out on street, receptionist? I mean look at us.

'Go on so,' she says.

Standing in very festively strewn canteen. Nelson dressed as Santa. Kids in queue meet Santa get chocolate. Get into queue with Charlie. He's a bit big for this but playing along which is helpful. Our turn. Nelson looks up me.

'Martin? I didn't know you were—'

'Was in the area, David. And thought we would just, stop in—'

He's looking at me, eyebrows up, and hard to tell if pleasantly surprised or quite angry due to cotton wool masking much of face. Expect latter. But too many people around and looking so cannot eject or cause scene as would look like Santa throwing man and son out. Would seem sharply at odds with Yuletide protocol.

'Right. Well. Just wasn't expecting … and who's this?'

'This is my son Charlie.'

'And how old are you, Charlie?'

'Eleven.'

'And what do you want for Christmas?'

Now right time to lean in and start the beg but Charlie pulls Santa/Nelson close to his ear. Charlie saying something to him. Can't hear what is being said. Charlie leaning in, low voice, reddish in face. Nelson putting hand on Charlie's shoulder. Saying something back to him into ear privately. Nelson puts his hand on Charlie's head and smiling at him. Lets him go.

Mood set somehow? My turn with Santa. Just get something. Anything. A partial commit. Will discount order by 20%. No authority to do so but we are well past this at close of play.

'David, I'm sorry this is terrible timing, but if there was any way you could—'

'It's OK, Martin.'

'It is?'

'I know what you're going through.'

Look over at Charlie. Has said what exactly? Should stay out of private business. But in fairness have dragged him in.

'Just tell James I said yes,' Nelson says.

'Yes to …'

'The whole order.'

'The whole order?'

Nelson puts out his hand. 'Done deal, Martin. Least I can do.'

Shake his hand and he puts other hand on top and am thanking him. Not sure what *least I can do* means at this point but not time to worry about details. Yes is yes.

He's putting his cotton wool covered mouth to my ear: 'You take good care of yourself.'

This all very unNelsonlike.

'I will. Thank you for this.'

Charlie standing away from us now and can see wants to get out of here and this mutual feeling.

'I should, well ...'

'Yes. You go. Spend time with your family, Martin. They're the most important thing.'

Possible he's been drinking or in full character but yes we should go get out of here before reconsiders.

Call James from car park.

'I can't believe it.'

Me neither but don't say this.

'So Nelson is a firm yes? Whole order for Q4?' he asks.

'Firm commitment.'

'How did you get the old bastard over the line?'

'Just, I think, caught him at the right moment.'

Wait while he tots it up.

'That puts you in the clear for Q4.'

As if have not done maths in head 49 times on way to car.

'Puts me over actually, a shade I think?'

'Yeah. Hold some of that back for next quarter. Jesus, Martin. Took it to the wire.'

And that is that. Q4 done. Zero variance. All problems, immediate ones at least, gone. Christmas back on.

Nobody going to die. Q1 starts in Jan and come last week March be in same situation but so far away no point thinking about future complications. And then remember small outstanding issue. Small matter of what did Charlie say to Nelson. Do not need to know. Private business between him and Nelson. Drive back, get tree, close this all out. Do not ask.

'Charlie. What did you say to him?'

'Nothing.'

'No, you said something.'

Charlie looking out window.

'You're not in trouble. I just need to know what you said.'

Charlie face with tear blur emerging. 'I said you had cancer.'

Ah. Damn. Explains easy close.

'What?'

'I said you had cancer, and all I wanted for Christmas was for you to not die.'

'But I don't have cancer.'

'You might. From smoking.'

'No, Charlie, I definitely don't.' As far as know. I mean possibly might. Maybe genuinely thinks I am dying. As talking of not feeling well and combined with radio talk, sick kids and so on. Couldn't have seen me smoking as was behind car and always hide it. But still knows. Knows what's going on. Maybe am dying and he has supernatural insight like canary in mine.

'Why did you say that? That's a ... you can't just ... that is – Jesus. That's the worst thing you could have said, Charlie.'

'You said you were in trouble at work and I thought maybe if he was sad about you he might say yes and you would not be in trouble and you would feel better.'

He is full crying now. Pull over. Christ. Need to go back and tell Nelson. Before he sends message to James/Nicki with confusing thoughts and prayers then further difficult conversations under Christmas tree and with HR.

'Charlie, I know you were trying to help me. But you can't just lie like that.'

'But you lie all the time.'

'Not like that. That is a, that's a very, extreme—'

'You said we were getting a tree and we didn't. You said we'd get something to eat and we didn't. You were doing work stuff the whole time.'

'We are going to do those things.'

'I was only trying to help you. You said you were in trouble.'

Look at him crying and this, wait, actually shining moment. This raising him from 7.5 to 9. In fact very helpful person and meaning well just using imagination. Will deal with Nelson. Now not time. Now time to say *don't worry I know it's OK I am not dying I know you were trying to help I will fix it it's not your fault.* Saying between hugs/tears which all passengers now have.

'Are you going to tell Mam?' he asks.

'No. I won't. If you don't tell her about the work stuff today. Deal?'

'Deal.'

Deal closed. Pull out. Keep driving.

'Where are we going now?'

'We're going back to the tree place. We're going to get the one you said you liked. We're going to put it up and cover it with lights. And we're going to have a great Christmas. That OK with you?'

'And get something to eat?'

'Definitely.'

Coming back into garden centre now and working on Q1 resolutions ahead of schedule. No more variances from promises. Remember you're being watched by Charlie and he thinks this is how you do it. This not how you do it. Starting in New Year or earlier if possible aim to not be endless unrealistic striving. Accept what is on offer and what already have, that's enough. Call Nelson say something like *Charlie has overactive imagination, we had minor scare but all OK now, appreciate if you kept private* etc. Not strictly a lie. Does have imagination and did have serious scare re target but all is OK now. And saying this way, protecting Charlie, not getting him in trouble: example of how to do it. If Nelson cancels order and Q4 short that's fair enough. If get actual cancer then harsh/ironic but as fair as anything else. Life not fair. Not life's fault. Call can wait until tomorrow. Resolve to get tree first. But Charlie right. Does not have to be most perfect amazing. Let him choose and get him home. String on lights, squint a bit: will shine fine.

ACKNOWLEDGEMENTS

EVERY WRITER (AND NORMAL HUMAN) needs a hand on the shoulder to hold them up and push them forward. I have way more than my fair share, and owe a debt to so many:

My family: my father Charlie; Robert and Caroline; and especially my mother Tish, true reader and believer.

My English teacher Joe Connell for turning a light on.

All who said there's nothing to lose, so why not try: Dan, Paul, Gillian, Mark, Steve, Matt, Edward, Martijn and especially John. Your friendship and support is treasured.

Sean, Declan and Danny at *The Stinging Fly*. June, Brooks and the brilliant CoFo Writing Group. Early readers, late-night reviewers, inspiring writers all day long: I'm so lucky you let me join your gang.

Francesca and all at *The White Review* for saying yes and opening the door.

My agent Sophie Scard for unwavering support and guidance, and an uncanny instinct for what works. Your trust in me made this happen, I'll never forget it.

My editor Charlotte Humphery for making every thought and word better (especially the ones that didn't make it) with patience and good humour, draft after draft. You and all at Chatto & Windus and Penguin Random House have my endless gratitude for taking me on and putting this in the world.

ACKNOWLEDGEMENTS

My day-job colleagues, especially Michelle, for letting me be out of office and up in my head awhile.

Dear reader, I hope you have such people in your life, saying yes and supporting you. I'm honoured to name mine, and to add you. Thank you for saying yes to this book.

Above all: To my wife Dawn, who saw this in me at the start and said go for it. You've supported me endlessly, through this and all else. I would not be me if not for you. To you and our three children, who are just on the other side of the door right now, while I'm in here scribbling: Thank you for letting me make this matter. Here at the end of a beginning (hopefully), and always, I'm thrilled to open the door and come back to you. To where, by dint of blind good luck and miracles, I belong.